MAY OF ASHLEY GREEN

Lilly Adam

Independent

ISBN-13: 9781542886109
ISBN-10: 1542886104

To my wonderful readers,
I hope you enjoy reading this book as
much as I enjoyed writing it.

ALSO WRITTEN BY LILLY ADAM:

Stella
Poppy Woods
The Whipple Girl
Rose
Whitechapel Lass
Daisy Grey
Beneath the Apple Blossom Tree
Faye
Secrets of the Gatehouse
Searching for Eleanor (Book one)
Loving August (Book Two)
Gracie's Pride

CHAPTER ONE

Cheshire 1860

"Let me go! Let me go! Get off me!" screamed May hysterically, as Bart Turrell's firm grip held on to her slender arms, as she desperately kicked and jerked, using all of her strength in the bid to break free.

"I must help my ma! Please let me go," she sobbed.

May's screams pierced through the smoke-filled November night, as the bright wild orange flames leapt high into the charcoal sky, leaving behind them a trail of destruction.

"Listen to me May," yelled Bart above the crackling of the burning timber, and the cacophony of raised voices coming from every direction of the hamlet, as men, women and children all took to filling up any empty vessel available from the nearby pond, and hurling the water towards the burning cottage.

"There's nothing you can do!" exclaimed Bart, "you'll be roasted alive if yer venture in there, an' someone 'as already gone inside to rescue yer ma!" Bart's words were of little comfort to May as she suddenly caught sight of her mother's body being carried out from the smouldering cottage, like a limp rag doll. As she was laid upon the cold and sodden grass, May felt the sudden release of Bart's strong hold on her as he fell to the ground. At that awful moment, time seemed to stop, as May witnessed her beloved Mother's face being covered. Her throat felt constricted, not allowing the terrible pain in her heart to be released out into the miserable black night. Her mother had not survived the fierce destructive fire, she was gone forever from her life, leaving her frozen in sorrow and abandoned.

Bart wiped away his tears with the back of his hand. The beautiful woman he had loved and admired for years had been ruthlessly taken from him in the prime of her life. All hopes of one day hearing her accept his continuous marriage proposals were now gone.

"I will love you 'til my dying day dear, sweet Emma," he sobbed under his breath, "you will live forever in my heart and no one will ever be able to replace you."

With her slender body, wracked with sobs, May collapsed to the ground as her legs gave way beneath her. Forcing her body to crawl to where her dear mother lay, she gently stroked her singed golden hair. Her beautiful, kind ma had gone. She would never again take comfort in her loving, protecting arms, or hear her gentle reassuring voice singing and humming, as she would every morning as she kneaded the dough.

May felt as though her whole world and her

heart had been completely torn apart in that short period. The cosy little cottage where she and her mother had lived happily for the past seventeen years was now just an empty burnt-out shell, blackened and deformed. There was no sign of the cheerful flower print curtains, that her mother had made, hanging from the windows. The delicate climbing rose bush which had framed the front door, and produced hundreds of fragrant blooms every summer, had now disappeared. May had lost everything.

"May Huntley!" shouted a familiar voice, "come on inside out of this cursed night!"

Mrs Weaver gently took her hand leading her towards the entrance of her home, after placing a warm woollen blanket around her shoulders.

Old Mrs Weaver, as she was known in Ashley Green was the oldest resident of the hamlet and had lived most of her life in the smallest cottage, not far from Emma and May Huntley's home. She was a treasure to all who lived in the hamlet, always ready to advise and assist in any possible way. Nothing was too much trouble for her, even now in her old age, when she suffered from rheumatism. She had a remedy for almost every ailment, and a solution for every problem, but she was never viewed as interfering or nosey by any of her neighbours. The children of Ashley Green never ceased to tease and taunt her, spreading rumours that she was, in fact, a three-hundred-year-old witch, only to suffer later when their parents felt the need to punish them for their unacceptable behaviour towards this true saint that they were fortunate to have residing in their quiet and peaceful hamlet.

May couldn't stop shaking as she sat at the square pine table in the warmth of Mary Weaver's cramped kitchen. Struggling to sip the hot tea she found it hard to believe the reality of what had occurred over the past couple of hours and hoped that she was just in the midst of an extremely bad dream. Her nostrils were still full with the strong stench of smoke, and glancing down at her calico nightgown, ripped and dotted with burn holes, she was reminded of how close she had been to not escaping the dreadful fire. Deep in thought she just couldn't understand why her poor mother had not managed to escape too...she had been right behind her as they'd hurried from their beds, but when she'd turned around at the foot of the stairs, May was unable to see through the searing hot flames and the dense black smoke. Her mother was nowhere in sight and there was no reply to her frantic calls. She was forced to flee from the heat and the choking fumes. Why had her ma suddenly vanished when she had been so close behind her, she thought, had she returned upstairs again, and why?

"Mrs Weaver," May cried out in alarm. "I must go to my mother. I must see her before she's moved."

"Now, now my girl," cautioned Mary, "you've 'ad a terrible shock, an' 'appen yer not thinking straight, what with all the smoke yer breathed in. Yer must try an' get some rest 'ere in the warm an' try an' calm yerself. There's nothing to be gained from going outside now, 'cept more grief an' upset an' yer dear ma, God bless 'er soul 'as more than likely bin moved already. You'll be able to see 'er in the morning after she's bin cleaned up an' dressed nice."

"But," implored May, suddenly realising that trying to convince old Mrs Weaver wasn't going to work. She would just have to sneak out by herself, as soon as possible, she thought.

"Now," she puffed, becoming quite flustered at May's request, "I'll go 'n' fetch a clean gown. Sure I must 'ave one in me 'bits 'n' bobs' cupboard, an' I'll fetch yer a jug of water so as yer can wash away that smoke."

Mary wiped away the burning tears as they rolled down her cheeks. She had witnessed some heartbreaking events throughout her life, but tonight had claimed her heart like no other. She knew now that Emma's lifelong fears and suspicions had become reality and she felt scared for the safety of dear sweet May. Poor Emma, she thought, that angel of a woman didn't deserve to be taken so young and in such an awful way.

"You just sit tight an' finish that tea." Tutting away under her breath, she slowly climbed the stairs.

Outside in the cold darkness, where the moon and stars were hidden behind a blanket of thick clouds, May could barely see her way down the narrow winding path, which led to her now destroyed home. As she ran barefoot, every sharp stone stabbed the soft soles of her feet, sending shooting pains through her body, and making her wince. An eerie silence had veiled the hamlet, which just a short while ago had seen all of its residents rushing around in a noisy commotion trying to contain the fire. As May arrived at the spot where her mother had been laid, just in front of the cottage, there was no sign of her.

"Oh no," she whispered to herself, "I'm too late." The sound of muffled voices coming from inside the cottage suddenly alerted May as she knelt on the grass, tears rolling down her cheeks uncontrollably, leaving clean trails upon her sooty face. Peering in through the darkness she could just make out the silhouettes of two figures, definitely men she thought, but these strangers were not men that she recognised from Ashley Green. As May's eyes became accustomed to the darkness she was able to see them more clearly. They were frantically searching through the burnt debris. The larger of the two, and the one doing most of the talking, suddenly struck his accomplice sending him crashing to the floor, yelping like an injured dog.

Startled and scared. May fled as fast as she could,

anxious to return to the warmth and safety of Mrs Weaver's cottage.

"Where 'ave yer bin?" questioned Mary sharply, as May stumbled through the door out of breath. "You'll catch yer death going out in this in yer nightgown and barefoot to boot, I owe it to yer dear ma to take care of yer!" Her face red and flustered, Mary bolted the door crossly.

"Now young May," she added, rubbing her chin, deep in thought. "I found a nightgown, not the best one, but it'll do for now. Go an' 'ave a wash an' put it on, then come an' sit down an' tell me what in the world yer was doing going out in the middle of this cursed night, an' what yer was 'oping to find out there?"

Sensing the seriousness of Mrs Weaver's tone, May decided that it would probably be best to do as she was told and keep on the right side of her. Suddenly overcome with emotion, May slumped to the cold stone floor, her petite shoulders heaving as she sobbed uncontrollably. It had been a long and stressful night, with the reality of it all of a sudden becoming apparent to May as she relived flashbacks of her dear mother laying lifeless, her beautiful body and hair burnt. Overshadowed by sorrow and grief, May knew that her life would never be the same again.

Awakening to the sound of crowing cockerels, May pulled back the faded curtain, only to be met by a view of thick fog. She could still smell the lingering smoke and in the darkness of the unfamiliar room, she knew for certain that she hadn't dreamt the events of the previous day. The narrow wooden framed bed was tucked in beneath the tiny window and covered with a thick grey woollen blanket, on top of which was a pretty but old and faded patchwork coverlet. At the foot of the bed stood a small pine chest, old, scratched, and battered but still serviceable. Balanced on top of it was a pretty green and brown floral jug with a matching washbowl. The room had a warm and cosy feel and was the only room upstairs of the cottage, which instantly concerned May as to where poor Mrs Weaver had slept and also to who must have carried her up to the room. Leaping out of bed, May hurried down the narrow creaky stairs. Bart Turrell's heavily built body swamped the small kitchen stool, as he perched awkwardly deep in conversation with Mary Weaver across the table, their tea, long gone, cold and forgotten.

"You've got to tell 'er Mary," he stressed as he twisted the end of his greying beard between his thumb and fingers, "If yer don't, someone else is bound to try an' get to 'er now that this 'as 'appened. She 'as to be warned Mary," he implored. "For 'er own safety...I don't like it, Mary, no, I don't like it one little bit."

Mary placed her finger across her lips, "Shhh," she insisted, "you'll wake 'er up with that great booming voice; just give me time, that poor young lass 'as bin through enough already. I'll tell 'er when the time is right."

Mary topped up the enamel mugs and drew back the curtain, "It's almost light," she sighed, "I reckon yer need to go an' get some sleep Bart, yer look in a bad way."

"Oh Mary!" he sobbed, "I might be able to close me eyes, but I doubt very much that I'm gonna fall asleep. My poor sweet Emma has left this world forever an' me heart hurts like nothing me words can describe."

Gulping the tea down in one swift gulp, Bart stood up scraping the stool across the floor. As he trudged towards the door, his head hanging low, he failed to notice May as she sat quietly on the bottom stair.

Pulling her rich chestnut brown hair out from under the tightly wrapped shawl, that she'd found at the foot of her bed, May sat silently observing Mrs Weaver as she collected the tea cups and brushed the table with the flat of her hand. Turning around, Mary took a sharp intake of breath as she suddenly caught sight of May,

"*Gawd 'elp us!*" she exclaimed, "Why, you be as quiet as a mouse upon those creaky old stairs, yer gonna 'ave to put some fat on that body of yours so as I can 'ear yer moving about before yer gives me old heart a shock!" Red-faced and flustered, Mary tried to be as calm as she could, not wanting to appear too feeble in front of such a young girl. She prayed that May had not been there long enough to hear what was said between her and Bart.

"Right, sit down at the table an' 'ave a cuppa tea, we've got a busy day ahead of us." Looking into May's deep olive-green eyes Mary took her hands in hers. "Yer dear ma is being laid to rest this afternoon my dear, so I want you to try an' be as brave an' strong as yer can," taking her hand out from her apron pocket she handed May her mother's wedding ring and the small silver pendant which she had always worn. "These are yours now." May struggled to hold back her tears, wishing that this was one long nightmare and she would soon awaken to life how it used to be. "Just 'ave a good old cry my dear," urged Mary as she held her close against her chest, feeling her despair.

"So why was Mr Turrell here so early?" questioned May, "and what must you tell me that's so important?"

"Well I never!" exclaimed Mary, "didn't yer ma, God rest 'er soul, tell yer that it's very rude to eavesdrop?" Shocked by May's question, Mary rattled her brain to come up with a feasible answer. She had been taken by complete surprise that May had overheard her early morning conversation with Bart. How much had she heard, she thought to herself. "Oh, nothing to worry yer sweet bonny head about, 'e was just letting me know about the arrangements and bringing those bits of yer ma's over."

The miserable cold and damp, November day only added to the bleakness of the graveyard. The longest and worst day that May had ever in her life had to endure, as she sobbed her final goodbye to her beloved mother, seemed to last forever. Even though all the residents of Ashley Green were also there, May felt strangely alone; with her neighbours seeming like a blur surrounding her. Feeling physically and mentally drained, it was a welcome relief to finally be on her own in her new, tiny bedroom, away from all of the well-wishers telling her that *'time would heal'*, and *'life must go on.'* May felt more like her life had suddenly ended.

CHAPTER TWO

Tom and Bill Haines sat miserably nursing their wounds in Boxwell's Black Bull tavern, their rough appearance going unnoticed in this dark den tucked away on the outskirts of town. Nervously pushing the empty tankard from one hand to another, Tom could feel the beads of sweat collecting in the furrows of his brow. The lingering stench of smoke was stuck to their rough and worn-looking clothes. They had travelled for days from London to Ashley Green to do a job and had failed to do it properly.

"We shouldn't be sitting in 'ere," whispered Tom nervously, "we could be recognised; we stick out like a sore thumb. I feel like we're being watched an' all."

"Just calm down won't yer, just act bloody normal an' stop whinging like a damn sissy before yer gives the bloody game away an' then we'll be swinging by the neck." Bill tried to hide the distinctive jagged scar, which ran down the left side of his face from above his eye to just below his lip, by pulling his long lank hair from under his cap to cover it. The scar made the entire side of his face puckered, causing his eye to look half closed and distorting his mouth. "Come on Bill," whined Tom, "let's get out of 'ere, me 'ands are killing me."

"Stop blowing on yer 'ands for God's sake, you

bloody fool," hissed Bill angrily, "come on, we're going." Scraping the chair loudly across the floor, Bill stood up and left the tavern, knowing that his pathetic younger brother would tag behind in his footsteps. He had always thought that Tom should have been born a girl; he had no backbone, was scared of his own shadow, and tonight had proved that he was unable to carry out a simple job without blowing it. Why had he brought him up here with him, he thought to himself. If he'd had left him back in London the job would have been done good and proper and he'd be returning to claim his reward, instead, the job was only half done, and Kingsley wouldn't pay up until both of those Huntley women had snuffed it.

"What we gonna do now?" uttered Tom as he hurried to keep up with his brother as he headed out of town towards the dark safety of the surrounding countryside. "Where are we gonna bed down for the night, we need to get some kip, an' me 'ands are really killing me, they're getting worse."

"Can't you bloody shut up for one minute about yer 'ands yer damn sissy!" shouted Bill, becoming angrier with every step he took, "you ain't the only one who's burnt and tired. If it wasn't for your stupidity we wouldn't be in this mess, and we could be heading 'ome to claim our reward!"

Tom hung his head and continued to follow Bill. His legs and head ached, his hands were stinging from the many burns which covered them, and his throat felt like sandpaper. Wishing too that he hadn't accompanied Bill on this job, he decided to keep quiet and save his ears from the usual verbal abuse that his brother always dished out to him. He had only wanted to prove that he wasn't the weak and feeble brother that Bill was always accusing him of being. That he too could be brave and courageous even though he was thin and scrawny and his body wasn't covered with bulging muscles as was Bill's. But if he had known that this job, unlike all the other escapades which Bill was normally involved in, was a job of this nature he wouldn't have set one foot outside of London. He didn't want to be associated with murder.

"Look!" exclaimed Bill, pointing out across the field to what appeared to be an old derelict barn, "that will do for the night, let's go an' 'ave a look." Wading their way through the tall dried-up golden bracken they finally reach the barn. Many of the wood panels were either missing or rotten, it was a miracle that this huge wooden shed was still standing, but at least they would be out of sight and sheltered. There were no leftover bales of hay inside, only a musty-smelling, damp and dirty floor which would have to do for the night. The brothers were past caring, both being desperate to sleep. Tom slumped upon the floor, leaning against the side wall, hoping that none of the loose wooden panels would fall and knock him unconscious in the night.

He was freezing cold, apart from his hands which

were burning painfully, and he couldn't stop his teeth from chattering violently. Looking at Bill who had laid down nearby and was already breathing heavily, Tom felt the bile rise into his throat. How could he have taken on such a job, he thought, poaching and stealing were fine, but murder...he moved his blistered hands to his throat almost feeling the noose tighten around it, constricting his airway. No, he thought angrily, tomorrow he would try his best to convince Bill that they should leave this area before they were caught, to hell with the reward. One death on his hands was too much to cope with, at least it hadn't been cold-blooded murder, there's always somebody losing their life in a house fire, he thought, trying to ease his troubled conscience. The sound of Bill's snoring echoed through the draughty barn as Tom struggled to sleep, terrified that if he did, he might not wake up again.

Morning arrived bringing with it a dense fog which hovered above the hedgerows. Concealed in the murkiness, Bill made his way back towards Boxwell, his rumbling stomach forcing him into a march. He had left Tom in the barn, whimpering in his sleep like a wounded dog.

Some food would soon cheer him up he thought, hoping that he would remain asleep until his return. Vaguely making out a faint light in the distance, he hoped there would be some easy pickings to be had. He'd spent his last few pennies in the Black Bull and his pockets were now empty.

His hands were covered with blisters, making him wince every time they brushed against his clothes, but he wasn't going to let a few burns get the better of him, he thought, not like Tom who hadn't stopped moaning and crying like a child, and was really getting on his nerves. What had possessed him to allow that baby to come along, he would have gladly handed him a cut of the reward if he'd remained at home, but he had begged him, and like a bloody fool, as always his younger brother had persuaded him that he was every bit of a man and would be no trouble to him. What a stupid fool he had been thought Bill, feeling every muscle in his body becoming tense.

Bill approached the light which was glowing dimly from a farmhouse set back a short distance from the winding rough track. Edging his way nearer cautiously, he could hear the sound of a crying baby and since the light was coming from an upstairs window he hoped that meant there would be nobody in the kitchen. Making his way gingerly around to the back of the house he noticed a small window next to the back door which was slightly ajar, not by choice but due to it being so badly warped it would no longer close properly. A slight grin came over Bill's face as the prospect of filling his belly lifted his spirits.

Sarah Milton paced back and forth hoping that the movement would settle and induce sleep in the tiny baby in her arms. Catching a glimpse of herself in the oval mirror hanging on the wall she felt shocked at how old and worn out she looked. Not quite thirty, the years had been harsh to her. Her once pretty youthful face seemed to have disappeared leaving a drawn and haggard appearance, along with the huge bags under her once sparkling blue eyes. Looking at Stan as he lay sleeping, she wondered if they would ever return to the happy days they had once shared as husband and wife before his accident and the death of their beloved firstborn. It was nearly two harvests ago since that awful tragic day which would torment her forever. She could still remember it as if it were just yesterday. Stan and young Jason had left the house early on that gorgeous bright sunny June morning; she could remember watching Jason, her heart filled with such pride at the sight of her tall, strong six-year-old son as he sat in the saddle while Stan led the horse out through the yard towards the bracken woods. That would be the last time that she would ever see her son alive. As long as she lived, she would never believe that the sounds which came from the woods later that morning, as she hung out the washing, were human. At first, she thought the distressing cries were coming from a wild animal which was fighting for its life. It was a deep piercing primaeval cry, causing a deathly silence to fall on the surrounding area and the sound of songbirds to abruptly cease. The sound then broke into sobs and Sarah instantly recognised her husband's distraught voice. A sudden coldness swept over her as she remembered that awful day. Stan had caught his leg in a vicious metal trap and was in agony as the snares' sharp metal teeth embedded themselves into his flesh. Jason had run to his aid, hollering and screaming at the sight of his father in such painful distress, startling the horse and causing it to rear up on its hind legs catching the side of Jason's head with a sharp blow from its front hoof. It was as if poor Jason's soul had been violently kicked from his dear sweet body as death came in an instant. Stan was bedridden for months after the doctor had amputated his leg just below his knee. On that one sunny June morning, when Sarah was so happy and content, everything had suddenly been destroyed. Two-year-old Jenny who had only just begun to string her sentences together and was a happy smiling child seemed to disappear into a dark shell, her smiles and chatter fading away. Stan couldn't see how he would ever be able to manage the farm anymore and blamed himself for the death of Jason. It was now up to Sarah to keep her family and the farm together, even though her heart was aching from the sorrow of losing Jason, she had to be strong if she was going to successfully run the farm and support her family through the difficult days which would lie ahead.

Employing workers from Boxwell to help with the harvest proved expensive. After selling the crops and the dairy products, and then paying their wages, they only just broke even. With Stan not well enough to undertake any paid odd jobs during the long winter months, Sarah became the main breadwinner, using her needlecraft skills, she sat up through the cold nights by the candlelight sewing beautiful gowns, which she sold at Boxwell's market along with the eggs and butter.

Sarah hoped that with the arrival of baby Adam two months ago, life would take on a new beginning for them all and Stan would be released from his long depression which was slowly destroying him, and he would stop blaming himself for the death of their son.

Adam had finally given in to sleep and as Sarah gently kissed his soft downy little head, and laid him back into his crib, she suddenly became alarmed at the sounds coming from downstairs. She felt her heart race, hearing the sound of the squeaking kitchen door being opened.

"Stan!" she whispered sharply." Wake up; there's somebody downstairs. *"Stan! Wake up."*

By the time Stan had limped out of bed and down the stairs, Bill had already helped himself to what he could find and armed with some bread, a tiny piece of cheese and a jug of milk, he was making his way hurriedly back towards the barn. The fog was showing no signs of lifting, making an ideal cover, he thought to himself as he crammed a large chunk of bread into his mouth, dribbling down the front of his already filthy coat as he chewed, and puffed out of breath while running out through the farm yard.

"Dammit!" yelled Stan, slamming the kitchen door shut and slumping down at the table. "If I were a proper man, I would 'ave caught that thieving bastard!"

Hurrying towards an old tea caddy, hidden behind the row of old but shiny pots and pans, on the kitchen shelf, Sarah breathed a sigh of relief on seeing that the small amount of savings they had was safe and untouched.

"Well," sighed Sarah, sitting down at the kitchen table next to Stan, "it looks to me like whoever that was, was just hungry, the loaf of bread has disappeared along with the last piece of cheese...Oh, and that small blue milk jug is missing too."

"Ma!" cried a small voice from the stairs, "what's all that noise...I'm scared." Jenny stood in the doorway, gingerly peeping into the kitchen as she rubbed her sleepy eyes.

"Come on over here, my sweetheart," voiced Stan softly, with his arms outstretched towards his young daughter.

"I think we could all do with a nice hot cup of cocoa," suggested Sarah, smiling at Stan and Jenny.

"I'm hungry Ma; can I have some bread with my cocoa please?"

"Well, I'm afraid that we only have yesterday's stale crust until I do the baking."

"Oh no," exclaimed Jenny, with a worried look about her. "What will my chooks eat for breakfast

if we eat all of their food?"
Stan and Sarah shared a smile, touched by their daughter's kind thoughtfulness on this very strange morning.

Bill was feeling much better, now that he'd filled his stomach. Looking down at the small scraps in his hands that he'd saved for Tom, he told himself that his brother always ate less than him and that this small helping would be plenty. He couldn't wait to return to the cover of the barn and rest his weary legs. That had been a close call, he thought to himself, that farmer could easily have caught him red-handed if he'd chased after him, or maybe even taken his gun to him. Seemed like luck was on his side this morning, he thought, smiling smugly. Entering the gap at the side of the barn, where the door had once hung, Bill was feeling pleased with himself that he'd managed to save a little food and milk for Tom, which he could easily have eaten.
"Wake up you lazy sod," he shouted, walking over to the corner where Tom was curled up in a ball and shaking violently. Placing his hand on Tom's forehead, he felt his brother burning up with a fever. "Oh God," he cried, "you've been a bloody pain in the neck since we left London, and now you're ill!" He placed the milk jug to his parched lips while giving him a slight kick in his side. "Drink this up," he ordered, lifting his head in an attempt to pour the cold liquid down his throat.
"I'm freezing, g...g...g...get me a blanket, an' tell Ma

ter put some m..m...more c..c..coal on th...the fire!" Carrying Tom in his arms, Bill struggled, staggering along the track, back towards the farm. The low hazy sun was trying to burn through the fog, and shining in Bill's eyes. The heavy dew glistened on the wet grass, soaking through Bill's worn-out boots and freezing his feet. His whole body felt cold, and his legs ached as Tom became like a heavyweight in his arms, "Don't you bloody die on me now, cos our ma won't never forgive me, nor will she believe that you begged me ter let yer come 'ere with me," shouted Bill in a state of panic as he stumbled along the pathway.

CHAPTER THREE

Arriving at the entrance to the farm, the place looked much different to Bill in the light of day. The chickens were scratching around in the yard, as a small child stood feeding them. The smell of freshly baked bread which was wafting in the air caused Bill's stomach to begin rumbling again. The farm looked old and run down with flaking green paint hanging from the wooden window frames, most of which had been boarded up, with many of the smaller windows being cracked. An old abandoned plough had been left to rot at the entrance next to a large gate which was hanging off on one hinge and an array of rusty broken tools and utensils were piled up next to a crumbling wall. The sound of continuous banging in the distance made Bill glance up towards the horizon where he could just make out the sight of a man hammering forcefully at a fence post.

As Bill neared the farmhouse the small girl suddenly dropped her basket of chicken feed and ran, sending the hens squawking noisily and running off in every direction.

"Ma! Ma!" yelled Jenny, almost tripping over the doormat into the kitchen.

"What on earth is wrong?" exclaimed Sarah, quickly wiping her flour-covered hands on her apron as she rushed to Jenny's side,

"There's a huge, giant man outside, he's really scary, and he's carrying a dead body...I think he's going to kill us too, Ma!" shouted Jenny, her huge round eyes staring at her mother in alarm. Before Sarah had the chance to think straight, Bill was standing outside the back door shouting for help.

"Quick as you can, Jenny," voiced Sarah, trying to sound as calm as she could so as not to frighten Jenny anymore, who was still feeling nervous after the break-in that morning. "Run up to the top field and fetch Pa."

Opening the door, Sarah eyed the scruffy-looking intruder, shocked at his disfigured face. Jenny fled past them sprinting as fast as her small legs would take her up to the top field. Stan was busily fixing the neglected broken fencing intending to secure the farm. The events of that morning had made him determined to change a few things in his life. It was time to stop feeling sorry for himself and to lift the heavy burden he had placed upon his dear wife. She had suffered enough; God knows what would have happened to him without her patience and determination to keep the family and the farm together as best as she could, he thought to himself. No, it was high time he became the man of the house again and took control of everything before it was too late. Sarah deserved a far better life than this, and poor little Jenny had suffered too; she was such a nervous child and had experienced too much sorrow and hardship in her four short years. He didn't want baby

Adam growing up pitying him either, no, he would be a Father to be loved, admired and respected, he thought, slamming the hammer down harder with every positive thought.

Catching the sound of Jenny's voice shouting, he stopped his work to look down the slope of the field. Placing his hand above his eyes to shield them from the low morning sun he could see the anxious look on his young daughter's face,

"Pa! Pa! Pa!" she was screaming, "Ma's in trouble, there's a horrible man Pa...you've got to come, quick!"

Dropping his hammer to the ground, Stan hurried as fast as his disability would enable him, to meet Jenny halfway down the slope.

"What...who... tell me who's there?" he puffed, taking hold of Jenny's small hand as they hurried towards the house.

Bill was already standing inside the kitchen when Stan and Jenny reached the house. He had laid Tom on the long wooden settle at Sarah's request and was hovering over them, his eyes slyly scanning the kitchen. The overwhelming stench of their unwashed bodies together with the smell of smoke which had clung to their filthy clothes had overtaken the sweet smell of freshly baked bread.

"Can yer do anyfing for 'im Mrs," Bill demanded in a gruff voice. Noticing Stan limping towards them, it dawned on him why he'd been so lucky and not been caught earlier that morning. Realising that Stan was suspiciously glancing at his pocket, he quickly pulled out the empty jug and handed it to Stan.

"Found this outside on the track," he declared, "thought it might belong to someone 'ere." Taking the jug from him, Stan caught sight of Bill's burnt and blistered hands,

"What's happened to you; looks and smells like you've come from a bonfire?" Stan enquired, feeling very uncomfortable at having these two unsavoury, rough-looking men in his home who were potentially endangering his family. Jenny had already run upstairs, where, Stan thought, she would most likely be guarding her baby brother who she adored, and was thankfully still fast asleep. Sarah had already covered Tom with a blanket and put a cold wet cloth on his head to try and break his fever. Feeling quite nervous and intimidated by these two strangers inside her home, Sarah thought it best to try and help them as best she could so that hopefully, they would soon leave.

"This is me little brovver, Mister," announced Bill, shuffling from one foot to another, "we've come up from London, on our way ter see our dear old grandma in Chester an' we was set upon by a gang of robbers...took every penny we 'ad they did an' left us fer dead. Then ter top it, me stupid brovver tried to light a fire in an old barn we was sleeping in, an' being the dim wit 'e is, set the place on fire." Stan eyed him suspiciously not believing one word of his story. These two dirty vagabonds were not to be trusted, thought Stan, and the sooner he got them out of his house, the better. "We ain't eaten in ages either," Bill suddenly declared.

Thinking along the same lines as his wife, Stan thought it would be in their best interest to try and help these two brothers, if they even were related at all, and send them on their way. Stan was no match for this heavily built rogue who towered over him and looked like, he made a habit of using his fists.

"Would you like to go and wash?" said Stan casually. "There's a pump outside, in the yard. None of us has had any breakfast yet, we're just waiting for the loaf to cool down a bit, and then we can all eat."

Stan and Bill sat around the kitchen table; Sarah had sliced the loaf and fried some eggs. As the steam from the enamel mugs of hot tea rose into the air, Bill's head was bowed over his plate, all worries of his brother suddenly gone, as he busily shovelled the food down his throat noisily, dripping egg yolk onto the front of his coat. Wrapping a slice of the warm bread in a cloth, Sarah quickly took it upstairs to Jenny, who she knew would be too frightened to show her face again while these strangers were under their roof. Sarah had lost her appetite and began clearing the table, removing the remains of the loaf before Bill consumed the lot. Not wanting to leave Stan alone with Bill, Sarah busied herself in the kitchen. The stench coming from these two intruders was making her feel sick. Oh dear God, she thought, why had they turned up at their doorstep?

"That were right tasty Mrs," exclaimed Bill, wiping away the crumbs and bits of egg from his grubby-looking beard with the back of his hand. "Ta very much, nothing like a good breakfast to start the day eh! Well, that's what our ma always says. As soon as me little brovver wakes up we'll be on our way; 'e's looking better already."

"Oh I doubt he'll be well enough to travel for a day or two," said Stan, walking over to where Tom was sleeping. This scrawny-looking figure of a man, whose putrid smell was overtaking the kitchen, was in a very bad way, thought Stan. "There's an empty store room just across the yard," said Stan, "you and your brother can rest in there 'til he's feeling better." Bill's beady eyes lit up on hearing this offer, feeling a sense of relief; this would be an ideal, out-of-the-way, hiding place he thought and would give him time to work out his next plan, plus with the bonus of this farmer's wife's cooking. He gladly accepted Stan's offer. "You can take a few bails of hay from the barn to sleep on and my wife will fetch some blankets for you," added Stan.

"Ahh yer a real gent, Mister," replied Bill, smiling broadly, displaying his array of black and broken teeth. "An' since we ain't got no money ter give yer Squire, 'ow about I lends an 'and 'elping out 'round the place? I'm a dab 'and at fixing things up."

"I was thinking the very same thoughts," agreed Stan, trying to sound authoritative.

Although relieved that the intruders would be out of her home, Sarah knew that having them just across the yard would put a strain on her family and she doubted that any of them, apart from baby Adam, would sleep soundly at night or be relaxed during the day. She knew that her disabled husband was no match for the rough and threatening-looking Bill and prayed that they would not harm her family in any way, and be on their way as soon as possible.

CHAPTER FOUR

In those first few very painful days after Emma Huntley was laid to rest, Mary Weaver made it her main aim to ease and comfort May in these early days without her mother. Days were short and becoming much colder with a sharp frost setting in every night along with freezing fog. They spent most days inside trying to keep warm and preparing hearty soups and stews. May contributed to the baking by making loaves, scones and tasty teacakes, all of which her mother had taught her. The upstairs room was now officially May's bedroom and had been cleared of Mary's lifetime assortments of bits and bobs to make more space. Mary had taken to sleeping on a bed made up on the wooden settle downstairs for the past few years to save her the agonising climb up and down the stairs every day.

"My bones aren't what they used to be," she would say," They just ain't moving with me body no more!"

May had noticed that with the arrival of the cold and damp weather, Mrs Weaver's aches and pains had become progressively worse, hindering her movement around the cottage. Bart Turrell would call most days, bringing with him the occasional rabbit which he had snared or a handful of vegetables grown locally, and making sure there was always enough chopped firewood.

Since his wife had died of pneumonia nine years ago, he and Mary had struck up a strong and trusting friendship. Bart's only surviving son, Jack, lived and worked some ten miles away at Fern Hill Farm for most of the year; returning home during the winter months to be with his father. This had now become Bart's favourite time of year and he waited with great anticipation and savoured every precious minute spent with Jack.

May sat by the fireside, busily engrossed in her needlework, altering one of Mrs Weaver's dresses to fit her. There had been nothing left to salvage from the fire, but due to the kind generosity of the women living in the hamlet, along with Mrs Weaver's donations, May now had more dresses and shoes than she'd had in her life, most of them requiring alterations to fit her slender figure.

"Put that down for a bit my love," said Mary, as she sat down next to May placing a tray of tea and fruit buns down on the side table. "It's about time we 'ad a little chat."

May felt suddenly alarmed, she had sensed this little chat coming for days now, ever since she had overheard some of the conversation between Mary and Bart on the night of the fire.

Was she going to be told that she had to leave, she thought, where would she go...it would surely mean the dreaded workhouse. Oh, God no, she mused, she would run away...anything, but not that place. Sensing May's thoughts and noticing her face becoming suddenly ashen, Mary felt a wave of protectiveness towards this gentle girl who was trying so hard to put on a brave face.

"Don't you go worrying yerself too much now," Mary reassured her, "and remember this, whatever 'appens, I'm always gonna be 'ere to 'elp you, and I'll do whatever I can for yer, fer as long as I live."

May now realised that what she was about to hear was to be a matter of great seriousness.

"Shall I pour the tea?" asked May.

"No my love, let it soak a bit longer, nothing worse than a weak brew."

May placed her needlework on her lap as she turned to face Mrs Weaver.

"I remember that day all those years ago when yer dear ma, God rest 'er soul, turned up at Ashley Green, with you just a babe in arms. Yer couldn't 'ave been much more than a few weeks old if I remember correctly. It was a glorious baking hot August day, one of those endless days where the nights is as warm as the days, an' everyone sets about washing their curtains and blankets, taking advantage of the heat. The roses were in full bloom, their beautiful perfume filled the air, the grass 'ad dried up an' turned yellow since we'd 'ad no rain for weeks an' the chooks were getting restless and puffing with their beaks open...they don't like too much sunshine yer know. Anyway, I remember looking at yer ma, standing there just by the pond, she was wearing a beautiful sky blue dress with a white pleated yoke, edged with fine lace, an' she wore a smart navy bonnet with the same lace trimming, an' a wide silk blue ribbon tie. She must of 'ad 'er 'air tucked up 'neath the bonnet, but I remember thinking to meself as I looked into 'er huge sapphire blue eyes, I bet she as 'air like the golden summer wheat, an' I was right yer know, well, of course, yer know. Pour the tea now my dear, we don't want it ter stew do we," she remarked, coming slightly out of her reverie, "now, where was I? Ah, yes, yer dear ma; she was a beauty, like a shining golden nugget turning up out of the blue in the hamlet." May wiped away a falling tear from her cheek. "And there you were in 'er arms, you were so tiny, yer just fitted perfectly into one of 'er arms and in the other one she was carrying a red and gold flowery carpet bag, an' I guess, all that she owned in the world. I invited 'er in for some cool, freshly made, lemonade that I'd just made. I thought she might like to freshen up and maybe put yer to 'er breast. Well, we got chatting, an' she told me 'ow yer father 'ad drowned at sea a few months back and that 'er father-in-law 'ad given 'er the cottage at the end of the hamlet as a sort of promise that 'e 'ad made to his son to look after 'er in the event of 'is passing." May rubbed her forehead, having a confused look on her face and then gulped down her tea which was fast becoming cold.

"But I know all this," exclaimed May, "Ma told me about my pa and my grandpa a long time ago."

"Did yer ever get to meet yer grandpa?" questioned Mary.

"Well, no...Ma always said it was too far away, and she didn't like London, said it was dirty and that you couldn't trust anybody there."

"Truth be told, my love," said Mary gravely, "when I 'eard what she told me, I 'ad me suspicions that it were the truth, but I'd only just met 'er. Such a lovely young woman, God rest 'er beautiful soul, so I bided my time an' 'elped 'er settle into 'er new home."

May topped up the tea cups, placing a bun on a plate for both of them. Still feeling confused and apprehensive as to where this conversation was leading, and why it was such an urgent matter. She wished that Mrs Weaver would hurry up and reach what she could only imagine was going to be some kind of awful confession. "Right, back to our conversation," muffled by the half-eaten bun still being chewed, Mary settled back with a long sigh. "Yer know, I got ter know yer ma really well. She were like the daughter I never 'ad, an' I like to think that I was like the mother that she never knew. Yer must 'ave noticed 'ow you an' yer ma's looks were completely different...hair an' eye colour, build...there weren't anything in you which could be seen in 'er...Did yer never question that?" Glancing at May's confused thoughtful face, she already knew what her answer was going to be.

"Ma always said that I was the image of my pa," exclaimed May suspiciously.

"Yes, I know she did," said Mary, "but she were just protecting you, my love."

"From what!" cried May, raising her voice.

"Now calm down my dear, she were yer ma in every possible way, and 'er heart was overflowing with love for you...you was everything she lived for, but 'ers wasn't the belly which yer grew in, nor the body which bore yer."

May's plate slid to the flagstone floor, breaking into pieces. This couldn't possibly be true, she thought, she would have known somehow. This was an awful lie that this old woman was telling her. Why was she saying these terrible things?

"No! That's not true!" she screamed, jumping up from where they were sitting. "You're lying, and she *was* my ma, *my real ma!*" The tears streamed from her eyes as she clenched her fists in anger and frustration. Oh, why isn't Ma here to put things straight, she thought.

"Come an' sit back down," coaxed Mary in a soothing voice. "At least 'ear me out before yer starts calling me a liar!"

May returned to the wooden settle next to Mary, eyeing her doubtfully.

"When yer were about three years old, yer ma got really sick with the fever, she was so bad that even the doctor didn't think that she'd pull through. But thank The Almighty; she eventually made a full recovery. During that time, I got Bart to carry 'er over 'ere into my cottage, an', of course, you, too; so as I could take care of you and nurse yer ailing ma.

When she were strong again, she looked like she were carrying the whole world on 'er shoulders, I'd never seen 'er so unhappy. Then one evening she confided in me an' told me the truth about 'erself; said that after 'er illness, someone 'ad to know, just in case....well, you know. Yer dear ma and pa were very happy, they loved each other dearly, an' they were in the employment of Sir Jeremiah Kingsley of Belgravia, London. Yer ma was the cook's hand and yer pa was a gardener. Ahh, it were a grand 'ouse by all accounts and in such a wealthy part of London. But then, one day, tragedy struck...yer pa was carried 'ome in a dreadful state, he'd been out visiting 'is ageing aunty who lived on t'other side of London, an' by all accounts, a terrible place, swarming with villains an' filthy little ragamuffins, whose parents, if they were anywhere to be found, didn't give a damn about 'em... poor little things. He'd bin robbed an' left in the gutter. The shock of 'im dying the following day, well, it made yer poor ma go into labour far too early, an' she lost 'er baby."

Mary paused for a while to glance at May. She could almost feel the pain that she was going through upon hearing this revelation. "You alright my love?" she asked softly, "Do yer want me to carry on, or shall we make some more tea first?"

"No," whispered May sadly, "please carry on Mrs Weaver."

"Well, that very same day, unknown to anyone in the Kingsley 'ousehold, Sir Jeremiah Kingsley's daughter was being born into this world, and unfortunately, not from the belly of 'is poor wife. No, 'e was a cad, to say the least, and 'ad put some poor naive girl in the family way, leaving 'er family to carry the shame...Well, that poor young girl didn't survive the birth, an' the little baby was left outside the trader's entrance to the Kingsley's 'ome in a basket, along with a letter from the young girl's family. She was found by the staff, an' before ten minutes 'ad passed it 'ad spread all over the 'ouse that the crying baby downstairs was Jeremiah Kingsley's bastard. All hell broke loose, but yer dear ma picked up that screaming baby, who probably 'adn't been fed since coming into this world, an' she gently put 'er on to 'er breast an' fed the poor little scrap. She told me as 'ow it felt like fate an' how much of a comfort an' joy you were to 'er in those black days after the tragic loss of 'er 'usband and baby. She truly loved yer from that very first encounter. It were yer father who bought the cottage and sent regular money to yer ma to take care of you. But just you remember this young May, as far as yer ma was concerned you were 'er daughter, an' no mother in the world could love 'er daughter any more than she loved you."

"So that's it," sobbed May, "I'm just a common bastard that nobody wanted!"

"Don't you ever say that," commanded Mary, raising her voice in objection, "yer name is May Huntley, daughter of Emma an' Henry Huntley, an' no one need know any different. You was the light of yer ma's eye, she adored you, an' don't yer ever forget that, *young lady*."

May gazed down at her lap; her needlework was now on the floor, along with the pieces of crockery which, thought May, was symbolic of how her heart was feeling, broken and in disarray. In the course of the past few days, her world had been ripped apart and now she didn't even know who she was. She was homeless, penniless, and now totally reliant on Mrs Weaver's charity.

"Please carry on, Mrs Weaver, I dread to think that this can get much worse."

Brushing away the crumbs from her lap, Mary let out a long sigh; she felt nothing but sadness and empathy for this dear girl who she held so close to her heart.

"About six months ago, Sir Jeremiah Kingsley passed away. Yer ma always knew that in the event of 'is death there would be trouble for yer both. Yer see, nobody knew of 'er whereabouts an' that he'd bin sending yer ma money every year, not to mention the cottage that he'd rented for 'er. Yer ma always knew that there would be something left for yer in 'is will when 'e passed on, an' she also knew that when that day came, there would be some sort of trouble. There ain't nothing like a will to bring out all the greed in folk an' all the worms from the woodwork. Years ago, she showed me 'er special hiding place behind a loose brick in the fireplace in 'er bedroom. A small metal safe box which contained papers an' documents...sort of telling who was who an' proof that you were Kingsley's daughter. Me an' Bart were the only ones who knew, so yer see, May, we reckon that fire weren't no accident." May's sudden sharp intake of breath startled Mary.

"That night of the fire!" exclaimed May, "I went back there. Do you remember? Well, I saw two men inside our cottage, I didn't recognise them as anyone from here in the hamlet, and everyone else had returned to their homes. *Who were* they?"

"Well, your guess is as good as mine, love," declared Mary, "but, I can tell yer this," she said smugly, "they never got what they was looking for, 'cos Bart beat 'em to it, an' it's now safe in 'is care. But those scoundrels, instead of being hung up, are out there on the loose an' won't be satisfied 'til they finish their job, proper like. We all 'ave ter be on our guard."

May swallowed hard, trying to fight back the tears. Feeling suddenly alone and scared, she knew that if she stayed in Ashley Green she would probably endanger the safety of dear old Mrs Weaver, who had been nothing but kindness itself and didn't deserve to be confronted by these ruthless criminals, especially at her time of life. What were these people capable of doing, she thought to herself, why couldn't they just leave her alone, she didn't want anything from the Kingsley fortune, besides, her father had never even wanted to see her since she had been born and now it looked as if her blood family were out to kill her.

May began cleaning up the mess on the floor and taking out the tray to the kitchen. Her head swimming with everything she had just heard. Mrs Weaver sat solemn-faced, the fire had nearly died down, and the light was fading fast. May returned from the kitchen with some firewood and a taper to light the candles. Noticing a tear rolling down Mrs Weaver's tired-looking face, it dawned on her that perhaps Mrs Weaver might prefer her to stay here with her, maybe she'd had enough of being lonely especially as she was growing older. Taking a woollen shawl from the hook on the back of the door, May placed it lovingly around Mary's shoulders.

"There's such a chill in the air, put this around you 'til the cottage warms up again."

"God bless yer May, it's like 'aving me very own angel, with you living 'ere."

CHAPTER FIVE

Quinton Kingsley paced back and forth in his study, stopping every few minutes to take out his pocket watch from his brown tweed waistcoat, a nervous habit he had when he was getting into a panic and life wasn't going his way. His large Havana cigar had nearly burnt down to his fingers, and a trail of ash covered the shiny wooden parquet floor. Glancing out of the window, he hoped that George Fenwick of Fenwick, Fenwick, and Montague would be in a compromising mood when he arrived. He had already managed to have the reading of his father's will postponed twice and would have to come up with a persuading and viable reason to put it off for the third time. Stubbing out his cigar violently he felt the beads of sweat running down the back of his neck as he clenched his fists so tightly, causing his knuckles to become white. How he'd love to use his fists on those Haines brothers he mused, wondering where had they got to. What a complete fool he had been to send those two ignorant idiots to run loose in Cheshire. Why hadn't he employed professionals to do the job properly? Would have been money well spent. Those two fools have more than likely ended up in Scotland...a knock on the door brought him out of his reverie.

"Yes!" he shouted, his voice unable to hide the

anger which was welling up inside of him.

"Enter!"

Gascoigne, who had been Kingsley's butler for the past fifty years, slowly opened the heavy oak door, its brass hinges giving off a drawn-out squeak, annoying Quinton further. Letting off a heavy, long sigh Quinton viewed the old stooping man standing in the door frame, waiting for him to speak.

"Well?" his voice boomed, almost making Gascoigne jump out of his wrinkly old skin. "What is it?"

"Begging your pardon, Master Kingsley," he said in a wobbly voice, still shaking from Quinton's outburst, "but Mr Fenwick has just this minute arrived Sir...should I show him in?"

"No!" replied Quinton sternly, "tell him I've had to go out on urgent business, there's a good chap. Oh, and Gascoigne, put some oil on those damn squeaky hinges."

"Very good Sir," said Gascoigne, thinking it very unlikely that Mr Fenwick had not already heard Quinton's rude thundering voice. How many times in his life had he been forced to lie through his teeth to cover up the misadventures of the Kingsleys' he thought, but at least the late Sir Jeremiah Kingsley had treated him with more respect. This young scallywag needs a good hiding; thinks he can walk over everybody. No, he thought as he returned to the entrance hall to deliver the message to Mr Fenwick, it's high time that I hung up my butler's hat and retired, spend my final years living peacefully in the countryside maybe, away from the filth of London, and without going to meet my Maker with liar written all over me. I've got a good idea of what he's up to.

Gascoigne could still remember that day as clear as crystal when Jeremiah Kingsley's illegitimate baby was left outside the tradesmen's entrance. He had witnessed the effect that the whole sorry business had had on the lovely Lady Annabel, she had never been the same again after that, it was as if she had just given up on life, no longer having any enthusiasm about the goings on in this fashionable part of London, or attending any of the many balls which had always given her so much pleasure, nor bothering with the family anymore. It was as if she was slowly sinking into a dark and gloomy hole. She ceased to eat or socialise with her husband or son, who was just a mere young boy of twelve years. Then when she contracted influenza three years later, it seemed like she had lost the will to live and fight the illness, allowing the fever to take a strong and tragic grip on her frail and malnourished body until it stole her last breath. It was lucky for Jeremiah Kingsley that the beautiful Emma Huntley had suffered the loss of her husband and baby within days of each other, and was willing to mother his bastard child, thought Gascoigne as he relived the turbulent times all those years ago, and now, that ungrateful good for nothing Quinton, who had never done a days work in his life is terrified that his half-sister stands to inherit a share when the will is read. There was only one reason why Quinton was desperately trying to stall the reading of the will and it was not something that he wanted anything to do with, he thought, shuddering at the thought of it.

Gascoigne returned to the study holding the oil can. Oh, how I'd like to squirt some of this over the floor and watch that spoilt, selfish brat slip over and knock himself out he thought....what had got into him? He'd never had such an evil thought in his head before, yes, he thought I must hand in my resignation. I've wasted enough of my life on the Kingsley family, and where has it got me?

Quinton continued pacing up and down in his study. Taking out his pocket watch, only three minutes had passed since he had last looked at it. He now knew how a caged lion felt. How was he going to stall Fenwick any longer, he thought, what was happening up north and why hadn't those idiotic, Haines brothers, returned? Maybe he could pay a visit to old Squire Hamilton, even though he'd not seen him since being a child, but since he was an old acquaintance of his late father maybe it wouldn't look too suspicious if he turned up there. He could tell him that he just happened to be in the area and couldn't possibly return to London without paying his regards to one of his late father's closest and dearest friends. After all, since Ashley Green was on the Squires' land there was more than likely going to be a mention in the will of him and the cottage where his father had sent his precious bastard child. Wiping the sweat from his brow, Quinton could feel his stomach knotting up inside; picking up the first object that came to hand he threw a heavy solid silver candelabra hurtling through the air, watching as it struck the shelf causing an avalanche of books to tumble to the floor. How could his father have been so bloody selfish he thought, why had he continued to supply money to that *Huntley woman* and the brat? Wasn't it good enough that he had secured them a home to live in and now after all these years, when all was forgotten, the dirt and the shame of the past were going to be dug up again, just making way for more humiliation. Why would his father want to embarrass him like this, he must have realised the trouble this would cause when he wrote his will. Why couldn't he just let sleeping dogs lie? His sweaty hands could hardly grasp hold of his pocket watch, it was nearly midday. Pulling on the bell cord to summon Gascoigne, Quinton hoped that he wasn't about to embark on a wild goose chase.

"Ahh, Gascoigne; pack me a small valise, I shall be going away for a few days."

"Very good Sir," replied Gascoigne, glancing down at the untidy pile of books on the floor, "would Sir be requiring an evening suit?"

"No Gascoigne, I want as little as possible, I'm

travelling light this time."

"Very good Sir," mumbled Gascoigne, feeling relieved that Quinton would be out of the house for a while. "Is there anything else Sir?" he inquired. "Will Sir be requiring the carriage, perhaps?"

"No Gascoigne, I'll hail a cab, now hurry up, there's a good man, I'm hoping to catch the one-thirty train from Euston station. That would be the one-thirty train today, not tomorrow," he stated sarcastically.

Quinton arrived in Liverpool tired, hungry and with no real plan of action in his head, even though he'd had the whole six-hour journey to think of one. It was nearly eight O'clock he noted, taking out his pocket watch. There was a strong northerly wind blowing, bringing with it a torrential downpour of icy rain, soaking through his outer clothes, chilling him to the bone and causing him to feel even more miserable. As he hurried along the path, a welcoming inn nearby lit up the dark deserted street, its look enticing him inside where he booked a room for the night and indulged in a hearty meal of meat pie, vegetables and hot bread, followed by a rich fruit trifle. In the morning he would make the journey to Squire Hamilton's estate in Cheshire, but for now, he thought, unable to suppress his yawns any longer, a good night's sleep was all that he required.

Sitting defiantly behind Quinton's dark mahogany

desk, Gascoigne blotted his letter of resignation, which he'd written with a great sense of satisfaction. He had decided to leave it on top of Quinton's desk to greet him on his return, by which time he would be well and truly away from the grand house where he had spent most of his life. Not intending to undertake another day's work, he would not hang about for a reference from his employer, nor for the two weeks' pay that he was owed. It would be well worth losing just for the satisfaction it gave him knowing what a state Quinton would be in on arriving home to find himself without a butler. He had saved enough money to rent out a comfortable room in a decent house in London, for the time being, until he had decided which part of the country would become his permanent abode to live out his final days. He intended to do a bit of travelling, make his way north and maybe visit Scotland for a spot of fishing and to enjoy the rugged scenery of the Highlands. He'd been the Kingsley's dog's body for far too long and was not going to spend his old age in the firing line of that ungrateful, lazy Quinton Kingsley, who was lacking in manners and decency. Gascoigne opened the top drawer of the desk in search of an envelope for his letter when he came across a document which caught his attention. It was the name, Emma Huntley, written on the front which made him curious. Scanning the document, he jotted down Emma's address. Maybe I could look sweet Emma Huntley up if I ever find myself in that neck of the woods he thought. So, that old scoundrel had packed them off to Cheshire. Frowning, he continued sifting through the papers being careful to keep them all in the correct order. He found what looked like a bank draft, and letters addressed from Squire Hamilton. So, he was in on this as well, he mused. These damn toffs thought Gascoigne, they're all as bad as each other, think their riches gives them the right to treat people with no respect. He then came upon an odd-looking paper with an East End address scribbled down on it, in very poor handwriting, which was signed B. Haines. Gascoigne had never heard of anyone of that name within the goings-on of the family and was overcome with a disturbed feeling as to why this should be amongst the documents which were all concerning Sir Jeremiah's illegitimate child. He put the paper into his pocket.

Later that day, after saying his goodbyes to a very shocked Mrs Booth, in the kitchen and the young maid, Lizzie, he left the Kingsley's residence for the last time, defiantly making his exit through the front entrance, without looking back. With a sigh of relief, for the first time in his life, he felt a sense of freedom and excitement, like that of a young schoolboy who was about to embark on an adventure.

Quinton had overslept and missed the train to Chester. Sitting in the mail coach, the bumpy road seemed to shake every bone in his body. The elderly man who was sharing the journey with him insisted on keeping up a continuous conversation even though he was practically stone-deaf. By the time he arrived at his destination Quinton's head was pounding and his throat sore from shouting. Taking tea and cake in a tea room in Chester's High Street before continuing on the next leg of his journey to Squire Hamilton's estate, it was a relief to sit in relative peace and quiet. Quinton would have liked to stroll around Chester for the afternoon, taking in the many historic sites, but knew he would not be received in the same welcoming manner should he turn up at the Squire's estate in the late hours. Purchasing a box of the best Havana cigars for the squire, Quinton travelled the eight-mile journey by hansom cab, keeping his eyes peeled just in case he should, by a small miracle see any sign of those crooks, the Haines brothers along the road.

CHAPTER SIX

"I'll get it!" shouted May, rushing to the door as Mary breathed a sigh of relief catching sight of Jack Turrell through the window. She seemed to be living on her nerves these days, finding it more and more difficult to relax and to sleep peacefully during the night, with the constant worry about May's safety.

"Jack!" exclaimed May, "come in, come in, it's freezing out there, oh, it's so, so good to see you again Jack, I've missed you so and I've been so, so..." Jack stepped over the threshold taking May, who was sobbing her heart out, into his arms, as he patted her soothingly on her back.

"Oh, God May," said Jack in a soft voice, "I heard what happened...I'm so very sorry; your ma was a good woman, the best, an' I know we're all gonna miss her so much. My pa's taken it really bad too, I've never seen him looking so down in the dumps, and forlorn; he's heartbroken."

"Come an' sit down by the fire son," ushered Mary, "it's like a breath of fresh air seeing yer 'andsome face again, we all need some cheering up."

Jack sat himself down next to Mary, unable to take his eyes off of May, *his beautiful May*, he thought. He hated to see her so upset, he would do anything within his means to comfort her and protect her from whatever danger threatened her.

In the eight months since he had last seen her, Jack couldn't believe how much she had blossomed. He had always thought of her as a younger sister, but today she seemed very different. Her dark brown wavy hair cascaded over her shoulders and framed her sweet rounded face, where her almond-shaped olive green eyes reflected the deep sorrow she was feeling. Jack had always thought that one day his pa and Emma Huntley would marry, making May his step-sister, so he had always kept his real feelings which he harboured for her tightly locked away in his heart. Now though, after his pa had felt it wise to explain to him the full story of Emma and May, he felt as if the key to his heart had suddenly been turned, setting it free after a sentence of captivity; free to pursue the young woman who held his heart. Maybe this was the reason why he was viewing her through new eyes, and why she looked even more attractive than before, he thought and wondered if May's feelings for him were merely that of a girl's for her older brother. Was it possible that she might one day love him as he loved and adored her?

Smoothing his hair down after removing his cap, Jack felt strangely shy and self-conscious of his appearance. He couldn't put a number to the number of times that he'd been in Mrs Turrell's cottage throughout his life, but today, he felt clumsy in these familiar surroundings and awkwardly out of place.

"Shall I make some tea Aunty Mary?" enquired May.

"What's that!" exclaimed Jack with a grin on his face, "I thought you didn't like anyone to call you Aunty...always had to be Mrs Weaver as long as I can remember!"

"Well, it's a far sight better than Grandma Weaver, which makes me feel and sound as old as the hills, and besides, May is family now, she ain't got no one else, so I'm to be 'er Aunty," explained Mary proudly.

"So can I call you Aunty as well?" teased Jack.

"No, yer certainly can't," declared Mary, tutting as she delivered a light slap to the back of Jack's head, "I'm Mrs Weaver to you, an' don't go forgetting that."

Becoming serious, Jack whispered into Mary's ear while May went into the kitchen,

" How is May bearing up Mrs Weaver, I'm that worried about her."

"Ahh, she's a brave young lass is that one, but I 'ears 'er every night sobbing into 'er pillow. Such a caring soul, she don't want to let me see 'er pain, but yer just gotta look into those eyes an' they say it all. How is yer pa coping now lad? Is 'e alright?"

"He's taken it real bad Mrs Weaver, been having nightmares, waking up in a cold sweat, shouting and hollering. He blames himself for the death of Mrs Huntley; reckons that if he'd insisted more and persuaded her to marry him, then those evil sods wouldn't have found them. With them changing their names to Turrell, it would have thrown them off the scent."

"Well son," said Mary sternly, "he's nothing but a fool if 'e blames 'imself. Some things are just meant to be."

"What's meant to be?" asked May, returning from the kitchen, with a tray in her hands.

"Ahh, just things that 'appen in life," sighed Mary.

"Are you back in Ashley Green for the rest of the winter Jack?" enquired May casually.

"Don't reckon that I'll ever be going back to Fern Hill Farm, not to work anyway," announced Jack worriedly. "The farm is to have new occupants, and they have such a large family that I'm no longer needed. Looks like I'm going to have to search for work elsewhere."

"Oh dear, that's such a shame, Jack." May tried her best to sound genuinely concerned, but secretly she was quite pleased that Jack wouldn't be returning to Fern Hill Farm and hoped that he would be able to secure work nearer home. She missed him so much while he was away, and longed to spend more time in his company. The endlessness of the summer days and evenings were always so boring without Jack around; he was the only one who could make her laugh, even when she was in the foulest of moods. May knew that from now on everything would be different and she would need Jack more than ever.

"Maybe yer could try for work on the other side of Boxwell," suggested Mary. "You know, the Milton's farm, them that lost their firstborn a couple of years back. I 'eard that the farmer's a cripple now, an' 'is wife's bin left to do everything, *poor woman*." "Maybe I could come with you Jack," announced May, "there might be some work for me too. Maybe I could help in the dairy or just help the farmer's wife with some odd jobs around the place. What do you think?"

Although Jack remained quiet, seeming deep in thought about something, Mary thought that it would be ideal for May to work away from the hamlet. It would distract her mind from the loss of her dear ma and hopefully take her away from the danger that loomed over her, here in the hamlet. Coming out of his reverie with a gleam in his eye Jack also warmed to the idea of working nearer home where he would be able to spend more time in May's company, and also stay with his pa all year round. Agreeing that they would both visit Milton Farm before the harsh winter months arrived, Jack stood up to leave, suddenly remembering the envelope that was safely tucked inside his jacket pocket.

"Pa said that you should have these now," he said, handing the brown envelope to May. "It's the papers that your ma had kept in her safe tin all those years. Pa had to throw the tin away, it was too badly fire-damaged." May was taken aback; this was the last thing she had expected to be given and would have preferred them to remain out of her life forever. If these papers didn't exist, her ma would still be alive, she wouldn't be confused as to who she really was, and she would be oblivious to the fact that her real father had been a self-centred womaniser who thought that his wealth could cover up and pay for his irresponsible mistakes. He had probably never even thought of her during his entire life, maybe there were many like her scattered all over the land.

Taking the envelope from Jack, her hands shaking slightly, she bade him farewell and went upstairs to put the envelope out of her sight until later, when hopefully she might have enough courage to go through it.

With hands pushed deep into his trouser pockets, Jack marched along the pathway, walking straight past his own cottage and onto the surrounding countryside. The graphite sky threatened rain and the few leaves remaining on the trees were struggling to hang on in the strong north-easterly wind. Jack leaned back against the trunk of a huge ancient oak tree, pulling his jacket collar up around his neck. He was unable to shake away the heart-wrenching images of May's saddened eyes from his mind. All he wanted to do was to wrap his arms around her and protect her forevermore. He desperately wanted to see her radiant smile on her face once more, and remembering how he could always make her laugh, he wanted to taste those happy times again, but he knew it would take time for her broken heart to mend. He wanted to shower her with beautiful precious gifts and provide for her every need, but more than anything in the world, he wanted to marry her and knew that if she refused, then he would spend the rest of his life unmarried and broken-hearted. He prayed that he wouldn't end up like his poor pa who had failed in his hopes and dreams of becoming Emma Huntley's husband. He would need a plan, he thought to himself, and the first part of this plan would be to secure himself with a job because without money, he wouldn't be able to buy May anything, let alone a gold wedding band. Yes, he would begin first thing in the morning.

By the light of the full bright alabaster moon which shone through the thin curtains of May's bedroom, she studied the contents of the envelope that Jack had given her earlier. She had given up the battle to fall asleep. Her mind was occupied and turning over inside like the cogs in a timepiece. In the attempt to decipher the many official-looking letters and forms, she concluded that any money which was being sent to her late mother would automatically cease in the event of the death of her father. Since he had passed away six months ago it now dawned on May that she was in a very sorry financial state, and if it hadn't been for dear Mrs Weaver welcoming her into her life as she had, May would probably have been taken into some awful workhouse by now. Scanning the letter from Fenwick, Fenwick, and Montague with its heavily embossed black ink heading, May searched hard through the long and elaborate-looking words trying to find ones which she could read or recognise, most of which she had never come across before in her life. Giving up with the paperwork, she wrapped her shawl tightly around her shoulders feeling tired and chilled and decided that she must look for work and earn some money to spend on herself and sweet Aunty Mary. It was decided, she would look after poor old Mrs Weaver, who had always been so kind and caring to her and her dear ma, and everyone in the hamlet. She deserved to be spoilt a little and taken care of in her old age. Tucking the envelope out of sight under her mattress May decided that she must try and get some sleep if she was to venture out to the Milton's farm in the morning. I wonder if Jack would like to accompany me there she thought, yawning as she rested her head and closed her eyes.

The following morning, May was woken up by the bright morning sun flooding through her window. Jumping out of bed and quickly pulling on her thick dark green woollen stockings and her brown serge dress, she hurried down the stairs being as quiet as she could so as not to wake Mary who was gently snoring beneath her patchwork quilt upon the wooden settle. Pulling on her boots and wrapping her shawl tightly around her shoulders she crept out of the cottage and hurried towards Bart and Jack's cottage, with her eyes fixed firmly on the frosty ground as she passed by the remains of her old home, not wanting to relive that awful night again. It was a lovely morning thought May, fresh but bright and sunny, just the way she liked it. She wouldn't mind walking on her own to the Milton's farm, should Jack not want to go with her. Tapping gently on the door of the Turrell's cottage just in case they were still sleeping, May didn't have to wait long before Bart opened the door, his warm friendly smile welcoming her,

"Good morning, young May, how are you today?" he inquired as he quickly adjusted his shirt.

"Good morning, Mr Turrell, I'm well thank you, as I hope you are too," replied May.

"All the better for seeing your bonny face," he said happily. "What brings you out so early on this chilly morning?" he asked.

Noticing that Bart looked as if he was ready to go out May quickly asked him if Jack was at home and how he had mentioned to her last night that he might be going to the Milton's farm today.

"Well, Jack left at the crack of dawn but I don't reckon he's gone there 'cos he took off in the opposite direction," replied Bart twisting his beard between his fingers. " But, if you are going over to the Milton's place, I can give you a lift on the trap on my way to market."

It was agreed, May accepted Bart's offer of a lift to the Milton's farm and within five minutes they were on their way.

CHAPTER SEVEN

Bill was busily helping Stan secure the two-acre field using all his muscle power to drive the thick fence post into the hard frozen ground. His lank greasy hair which hung over half of his face had a putrid odour to it which was causing Stan to step back every time the gentle breeze blew in his direction. His festering hands were still feeling the painful effects of the burns and were covered by a pair of Stan's thick work gloves. Tom had taken a turn for the worse, his fever hadn't shifted and the burns had become badly infected. He hadn't managed to get up on his feet since arriving at the Milton's farm and was becoming weaker every day. Bill was becoming increasingly tired of having to labour from dawn to dusk every day as well as having to take care of Tom, and all for a meagre meal at the end of the day and the use of an old freezing cold, damp, store room which even the rats had abandoned. He was also struggling to keep his temper as everyone was annoying him more and more with each passing day, and keeping up the pretence of being someone whose character was the complete opposite of his, was becoming very taxing. The kid was terrified of him and ran screaming in the opposite direction if they happened to meet. Pathetic, country brats he thought; the street kids back home were made of tougher stuff with only a few being squeamish at the sight of his deformed face. The farmer's wife eyed him suspiciously, often spying on him from behind the curtains. The only reason that Bill was stuck out in the middle of nowhere was because his idiot brother was the usual thorn in his side. Stan was also getting on his nerves too; always bossing him around as if he was paying him a king's ransom, yet he wasn't even allowed to set foot inside of the house; any food or cups of tea were fed to him outside in the cold like a dog, or worse still, sitting with Tom who continuously moaned and nagged him. Bill was just biding his time until the chance of stealing a horse and cart came his way and he'd be able to load Tom onto it, making a getaway to pastures new where he could plan how he was going to locate and get rid of that Huntley girl.

"I think it's time for a break," announced Stan, adjusting his cap, "then we can finish off all the fencing today, and tomorrow I want you to help me fix all the broken windows on the house, it's getting real draughty now, and I don't want the little uns getting coughs and colds."

"Right you are, Gov," agreed Bill, his hands tensing into fists, thinking how much pleasure he would get out of giving this man a good beating.

"How's that brother of yours today?" he enquired as they made their way back down to the yard.

"He ain't much better, always been a weakling 'as Tom, it don't take much ter send 'im to 'is sick bed," replied Bill, "but don't worry none, Gov, we'll be on our travels an' out of yer way as soon as 'e can stand on 'is feet."

The sound of cart wheels passing near the farm entrance made both Stan and Bill look to see who was arriving.

"Looks like you've got visitors," mentioned Bill casually, glancing with interest in the hope that this might prove to be the ideal opportunity for him and Tom to escape with this horse and trap, should it be left in the yard unattended.

Stopping briefly to allow a young woman to alight, the horse cart was soon carrying on down the track, the driver waving to the woman as she made her way to the farmhouse door. Not recognising the visitor, Stan assumed it was one of Sarah's many acquaintances. She had become quite a sought-after seamstress over the past couple of years, well known for her beautiful sewing skills, and was often given work from people in the surrounding towns and villages.

Bill walked straight towards the water pump in the yard and gulped down a ladle of icy cold water in his usual noisy fashion, pausing to spit out a mouthful of phlegm, half of which landed on his trouser leg. As Stan neared the house, he couldn't help noticing that the visitor was just a young girl, probably no more than eighteen, thought Stan, admiring her pretty youthfulness, which reminded him of Sarah all those years ago when he had first set eyes on her.

"Good day, Miss," called Stan, in a jolly voice. "Are you looking for Sarah?"

"Oh good morning," answered May, shyly, "I'm looking for Mrs Milton, I was told that there might be some work for me here." Noticing the man's limp, May knew immediately that she was talking to Mr Milton. He looked like a kind man, she thought, he had a friendly welcoming smile.

"Well, you'd better come on in out of the cold then and have a chat with my wife, I expect she's busy with the little un, otherwise she would have opened the door by now," he said, as he opened the door inviting her in.

Bill was still standing by the pump straining his ears in vain trying to hear what was being said. Thinking how pretty this young maid looked, his imagination had already entertained him enough, putting a distorted smile upon his grubby face.

The smell of freshly baked scones resting on a cooling rake and the warmth of the cosy kitchen greeted May as she stepped over the threshold. A small flour-covered girl was kneeling on a chair at the table in deep concentration as she tried to spread some solid butter onto a soft warm scone which had broken into pieces on her plate, not deterring her from cramming as much as she could into her petite mouth.

"Hello Pa," she muffled, her cheeks suddenly blushing on catching sight of May.

"Where's your ma?" questioned Stan, as he ruffled

her hair, helping himself to a piece of her broken scone.

"She's upstairs seeing to baby Adam," replied Jenny, quickly gulping down the mouthful of food, not wanting to look rude in front of this pretty woman. *"Pa!"* she suddenly exclaimed, "shut the door before the monster comes in."

"Jenny!" cautioned Stan, feeling slightly embarrassed at his daughter's announcement, as he glanced at May. "How many times have I told you, Jenny, people can't always help the way they look, now run upstairs and fetch yer ma, there's a good girl."

No sooner had he spoken than Sarah appeared in the kitchen doorway curious as to whom this visitor was, in her home.

"Ah, Sarah dear," acknowledged Stan, "this young lady has come to see you." Stan poured himself a cup of milk and went back out into the yard. Sarah straight away sensed a sadness about this slender young girl and was immediately taken to her sweet innocent face as she stood shyly smiling at her.

"Hello," said Sarah, returning a smile, "would you like to sit down, I was just about to brew some tea. I hope you'll join me."

"That would be lovely, thank you," replied May.

"Sit down next to me," implored Jenny, patting the seat of the chair beside her. "I like her Ma; she's got a smiley face and pretty hair."

Sarah and May both laughed at Jenny's declaration.

"There's nothing like a child's talk to break the ice and put an end to a nervous moment," stated Sarah.

"What's your name?" inquired Jenny, not taking her eyes off her.

"*Jenny!*" exclaimed Sarah, "what happened to your manners?"

"My name is May, May Huntley,"

"Oh," cried Jenny, "that is my favourite name in the whole world. Would you like to try one of my scones that I made...well, I helped Ma make them, but they taste del...del...delicious, even my pa says that."

May sat down next to Jenny, while Sarah was busy making the tea and brushing away the flour which had left a fine covering over the flagstone floor. Jenny had instantly taken to May and was busy chatting away telling her all about the really scary monster who was living in the store and then went on to tell her about her precious little brother who she would soon be able to take out into the yard with her to help in the feeding of the chickens. Sarah laughed when hearing this, explaining that baby Adam was only a few weeks old. Sarah took an instant liking to May, she was a gentle, kind-looking girl with a lovely way about her. She also had an honest and trustworthy face thought Sarah, and after chatting to her over tea and scones for just a short while Sarah felt like she had known May for years and that this was the beginning of something very special. May told Sarah that she had recently lost her ma, but omitted the details of exactly how she died and the circumstances surrounding the whole business, but told her that she now lived with her aunty. Although Sarah wasn't able to offer May any properly paid work just yet, she suggested that perhaps she could pay her in food to start with until the Milton's financial situation improved. Sarah explained to May how she made gowns and sold them at Boxwell market as well as receiving orders from customers, and how, if May could help with the dairy work and the children, it would give Sarah more time to spend on the dressmaking, hopefully turning it into a thriving business and then she would be able to pay May a proper wage.

"Maybe I could also help with the sewing," suggested May, "I could even take some home with me to work on in the evenings. That's if you don't mind of course. That way the gowns would get finished much quicker."

"That sounds like a jolly good idea," agreed Sarah, but not wanting to commit straight away, said, "why don't you come in for a couple of days a week to start with, you might change your mind after you've had to listen to Jenny chattering on all day!"

"Oh, she's adorable," laughed May, "I could chat with her all day long."

"Do you want to come and see my chooks now, May?" pleaded Jenny.

"I doubt that poor May wants to go and stand in the cold yard to look at the chickens," voiced Sarah.

"I'd love to Jenny," replied May, as she stood up placing the chair neatly under the table, "besides, I have to be on my way home now."

"Would you be able to come tomorrow for the day," enquired Sarah, "to help me out around the place."

So it was agreed, that May would return the following day.

Hoping that she wasn't too late to catch a return lift with Bart Turrell on his way back from the market, May said her farewells to Sarah, as Jenny escorted her across the yard holding her hand, in order to show off her beloved hens.

"Look," whispered Jenny, "there's that monster I told you about," pointing to Bill, as he was making his way down the field. May was shocked that Jenny's monster actually existed; she thought it had just been the child's overactive imagination. "I'm going in now," announced Jenny in a shaky voice, "he scares me....see you tomorrow, May."

Releasing her hand suddenly, Jenny ran like a terrified rabbit towards her home, leaving May feeling very puzzled as to why a lovely family would let someone work on their farm who their young daughter was petrified of. That would be something she would try and find out tomorrow, she thought.

With there not being any sign of Bart on the road, May began her long walk back to Ashley Green with plenty to think about on the journey. She was anxious to find out where Jack had gotten to that morning and couldn't wait to tell him about the job she now had at the farm. She had really liked the Milton family and little Jenny was such a sweet girl.

Being away from Ashley Green for the day had, for the first time, diverted her mind from the constant worry of her family problems, and if someone was trying to harm her, then being away at the Milton's farm would be much safer for her. Hearing the sound of cart wheels approaching, May turned around to find it was not just Bart, but sitting alongside him was Jack with a beaming smile to greet her.

"Look who I found on my travels," announced Bart, pulling on the reins and bringing the horse to a standstill.

"Jack!" exclaimed May, returning the smile. "Where did you disappear to so early this morning? I was hoping that you would accompany me to Milton Farm to look for work." Outstretching his hand to assist May onto the cart, he said in a mysterious tone,

"I've been making me own enquiries, and not on the Milton's farm, but all will be revealed in good time."

"Well," replied May, "aren't you the dark horse."

Jack tenderly placed a rug over May's legs as they continued towards Ashley Green, chattering away amongst themselves, with May telling them about her new job at the Milton's farm.

CHAPTER EIGHT

Like every other morning, Bill was awoken by the chattering of his teeth and by the pain from the cold which invaded every part of his body. The temperature was plummeting to well below zero degrees every night and the cold, damp, disused store room was no place to be spending the winter months which lay ahead. Tom sat up with just his cold red face peeking out from the mass of blanket that he'd wrapped around the top half of his body. He looked gaunt and pitiful, with his lean body just propped up against a bail of hay. Although his fever had now gone, his hands were a mess, covered with puss-filled, excruciatingly painful scabs which were refusing to heal and continued to bleed with every movement. His pathetically weak and puny muscles were wasting away and Bill knew that it would be impossible for him to walk out of this farm which had now become their prison, with Bill working like an unpaid slave all day.

"You awake, Bill?" questioned Tom,

"give us yer blanket while yer fetches our breakfast."

Bill didn't think that he would be able to take much more of this; he felt trapped and couldn't see a way out of this mess unless he could somehow get his hands on a horse and trap from somewhere.

"It ain't even morning yet," groaned Bill angrily,"
go back ter sleep."

"I can't, I'm bloody frozen and starving. I wanna
go 'ome Bill, please take us 'ome. Ma will know 'ow
ter make me better again," he cried. "I miss Ma, I
don't wanna die 'ere, I wanna go back ter London,
please Bill, take me 'ome." Bill stood up, throwing
his blanket on top of his brother in the hope to
keep him quiet for a while. Scratching his head,
he walked to the door, pausing for a second to
glance back at Tom. It was still pitch black outside
apart from the glare of the medallion moon. All
was silent and still. The ground was carpeted
with a thick white frost and the water pump had
frozen solid leaving crystal icicles hanging from
the spout. Bill could easily break into the Milton's
house but was reluctant to do so for fear of getting
him and Tom thrown out, but this morning he
didn't care. They were being treated like a couple of
dogs, being left out in the icy store room all night,
thought Bill as he crept across the yard. This would
be his last chance to gain access to the house so
easily as Stan had said that today they would begin
fixing all the broken windows and renewing the
hinges. Slowly opening the window and stretching
to unbolt the door like a sly fox, Bill was soon
standing inside the kitchen and staring head-on at
half a blackberry pie on the table. Grabbing the pie
and the now familiar blue milk jug, he swiftly left,
returning to the store room.

"Ere Tom, I got us some grub," he said eagerly.

Tom managed a small smile, but could only eat a meagre amount in between bouts of choking coughs. Bill handed him the jug of milk which he sipped in short spurts, spluttering most of it down his already-stained blanket. For the first time in his life, Bill felt genuinely sorry and concerned for his little brother.

"Don't you worry Tom, I'm gonna get yer 'ome, I don't know 'ow yet, but yer know me when I puts me mind to something."

"Ta Bill," replied Tom weakly.

Bill returned the milk jug and the remains of the pie to the kitchen, with a bit of luck he thought, they might just think that the mice were the culprits. Unable to get back to sleep, Bill rattled his brain to come up with some sort of plan or an idea of how to get him and Tom back home to London, but more importantly, how he would finish what he had travelled to Cheshire to do so that he could claim his due from that arrogant snob Kingsley, then he would stick to good old fashioned thieving and pickpocketing and maybe even settle down if anyone would have him. He'd have to snatch a horse and cart from somewhere or even just a hand cart. He wouldn't be able to carry Tom for long and it would bring too much attention to them. He had to find out which cottage the Huntley maid was now staying in, that's if she hadn't been carted off to the workhouse by now, and if that was the case, then his mission would be even more difficult.

He must have been mad to accept this job, he thought, he could be back in the streets of his familiar East End of London instead of this place, stuck out in the middle of nowhere.

Bill must have dozed off to sleep again but was soon awoken by the sound of Stan hammering on the door with his fists.

"Bill," he shouted, "got some tea and food for you out here."

Opening the store door, Bill took the two enamel mugs of steaming hot tea from Stan, and the slices of warm freshly baked bread which he had tucked under his arm.

"Everything alright Bill?" enquired Stan. "How's Tom today?"

"Ta very much, Gov," replied Bill, placing the tea down on the storeroom floor. "'e's still the same, Gov; half the man 'e used ter be, 'e don't seem ter be getting any better; reckon I should try an' get 'im 'ome somehow."

"I'll ask the wife what she thinks," said Stan, looking doubtful. "Have some breakfast and we'll talk about it later. I'd like us to fix the broken windows today Bill."

"Right you are, Gov, be out just as soon as I've drunk me, Rosie Lee...that means tea, Gov," he replied smirking.

Bill set to work straight away after returning the tea cups, leaving them outside the back door. As he chiselled away at the paintwork on the rotten window frames, Sarah, who was busy in the kitchen didn't like the idea of Bill working so near to the house.

"Can't you do that Stan," she pleaded, with a hand jester towards the window? "I don't like him so close by, and he can't be trusted. Let him work on the fields while you sort out the woodwork Stan."

"You know I'm not much good up a ladder Sarah with my leg, and I promise I'll be nearby. I'm gonna be painting what I can reach on the ground level while he does the upstairs windows. Now careful what you say," cautioned Stan, lowering his voice, "he can hear you while he's out there you know."

"But Pa, I'm scared with that monster outside!" declared Jenny looking up from her bowl of porridge, "and I know that May will be scared of him too when she comes today and she might not come back and she's so nice and pretty and she wears pretty dresses and she has shiny eyes and..."

"*Hay!*" exclaimed Stan, "calm down and finish your breakfast, my head's spinning with all your chatter young miss." Looking amused, Stan turned to Sarah for an explanation.

"You remember Stan, I told you last night or were you listening to me with your ears closed...the girl that came here in the day, May Huntley from Ashley Green, remember? She's coming over today to help me out around the place, and I think that *this one* is her biggest admirer," she said, pointing to Jenny.

Outside, Bill couldn't believe what he was hearing, and he couldn't contain the wide grin which spread across his grubby face on hearing this conversation. Had his luck suddenly changed, he thought. She was coming here! To save him the bother of hunting for her, she was practically being handed to him on a plate. As his spittle trickled down his filthy matted beard, he sanded the window frames with renewed vigour, feeling jubilant that he could now finish the job and return home, never to set foot out of London again for as long as he lived. So, he thought, that scrawny, weak-looking thing who was here yesterday was May Huntley, she would give him no problem, he could snap her skinny neck like a dried-up twig. The biggest problem would be to make a quick getaway with Tom being such a handicap.

Bill was brought out of his reverie when Stan suddenly appeared laden with rusty old tins of paint.

"Doing a good job there Bill, soon be ready for the painting. How's your brother? Any improvement?" he questioned.

"He's just pining to go 'ome, Gov," replied Bill cautiously, paving the way so there would be no suspicions if he was able to get everything sorted out quickly, and make a sudden getaway from Cheshire. "Reckon we might be on our way soon, Gov, you've bin most 'ospitable and me an' Tom is most grateful, Gov."

"So will you be continuing to Chester then....was it your grandmother or your aunty that you were off to visit, I don't seem to remember." Bill couldn't remember what he had told Stan on the day that they'd arrived but wasn't going to let a small lie bother him, after all, talking his way out of a tricky situation was one of his many skills, and he'd had plenty of practice.

"Well, yer see, Gov, I could 'ave said me grandmother or I could 'ave said me, aunty, cos they both live in the same 'ouse yer see." As usual, Stan didn't believe a single word that spilt from Bill's mouth; he was a born liar he thought, as Bill stood with a smug smile on his face displaying his grimy brown uneven teeth.

"Let's try and get some of these windows finished today," said Stan, wanting to change the subject, "by the look of those clouds up there, looks like we could be heading for a storm."

Inside the warmth of the kitchen, May began helping Sarah with her many chores. Jenny was so excited knowing that May was going to be staying for the whole day, but had been given a strict warning earlier that morning to allow May to get on with her chores and not to keep bothering her. By mid-morning, Sarah was in no doubt as to how fortunate she was to have May's assistance. She was so capable, seeming to be mature beyond her years and able to do every task that Sarah asked of her with confidence and ease. While Sarah went to the barn to milk the few cows that they had left, May set to the baking. Despite the warning that Jenny had received, she couldn't help herself chatting to May, and was delighted when May allowed her to help, listening attentively as May explained everything she was doing in detail to Jenny, just as her ma had taught her when she was a child. Later on in the day, when all the cooking was finished and Jenny reluctantly went for her afternoon nap, Sarah brought out her sewing box and showed May the latest project that she was working on. It was a beautiful powder blue, flowing, taffeta ball gown to which Sarah was now embroidering delicate leaves and flowers to the bodice, along with tiny white seed pearls. Adam woke up crying for a feed and May asked if she could continue with the embroidering while Sarah went to feed and settle him. Although she doubted that a young girl would be capable of such intricate needlework, not wanting to offend May, she agreed and was pleasantly surprised on returning from upstairs to see yet another of May's many talents.

"Did your mother teach you all of your amazing skills May, or are you just a natural born genius?" Blushing slightly, May told Sarah how her father had died before she was born and how her ma had been a skilled needlewoman and an exemplary cook, teaching all her skills to May. It was only since her ma's death that May had become aware of how skilled she was but had just presumed all girls of her age were just as capable as she was. She had received countless compliments when her neighbours had seen how she had transformed their 'hand-me-downs' into beautiful dresses, and Mary Weaver praised her endlessly, complementing her delicious cooking and continuously telling her that she would make some fortunate man a lovely wife one day.

May couldn't hold back the tears as she spoke lovingly of her dear ma, and as Sarah comforted her she was shocked to hear that it was so recently that May had lost her, and even more alarmed on hearing how she had died. Sarah knew all too well the feeling of grief and how it nestled in the heart like a heavyweight.

"Why is May so sad?" spoke a tiny voice, as Jenny appeared in the kitchen, rubbing her eyes and yawning. "Did you tell her off Ma?" As usual, Jenny's comments never failed to change the atmosphere, causing May and Sarah to smile.

Sarah insisted on arming May with a basket full of provisions before she left the farm that day. Bart had told May that he would be passing by the Milton's farm at about three-thirty and would wait for her there. May was pleased that her first day had gone so well, she liked Sarah Milton and dear little Jenny was a treasure. She couldn't wait to tell Mrs Weaver about her day and to give her the basket which had been filled with cheese and butter from the dairy, bread which May had baked in the morning and some carrots, beans and a cabbage from Stan's vegetable field. Jenny had put in two scones, one each she had said for May, and her aunty. After saying her goodbyes to Sarah and

Jenny and promising them that she would return the day after next, she made her way through the yard to wait by the entrance for Mr Turrell.

The daylight was diminishing fast, and the sky threatened rain with huge dark clouds above. May pulled her shawl securely around herself trying to keep out the cold air. Looking up and down the roadway, she hoped that Mr Turrell hadn't forgotten that he was going to take her home. Catching sight of Jenny's monster as he stood by the store room where, Jenny had told her, that he and his sick brother lived, she could see why Jenny was so terrified of him. She was sure he was just standing there staring straight at her, making the hairs on the back of her neck stand up as she shivered, becoming scared at the sight of him.

The sound of the cart was a welcoming sound. Thank God, thought May, as the horse advanced towards her. She was even more delighted to see that it was Jack.

"Jack," she exclaimed, "I, was beginning to think I'd have to walk home, you're such a welcome sight."

Jack could sense the fear in May's voice, and as he helped her up onto the seat he caught sight of Bill, and knew that his presence had disturbed May.

"Who's that strange-looking man, is he one of the Milton family?" questioned Jack as he gently snapped the reins telling the horse to walk on.

"That's little Jenny's monster, she's absolutely petrified of him, and I can see why. He's been standing there since I left the farm! I'm positive he's trying to scare me with his incessant stare. I really don't trust him. Apparently, according to Jenny, he lives in the store room with his sick brother. I know that Mrs Milton doesn't like him, although she hasn't said as such, but I can just tell."

"You make sure you let me know when you are working and I'll make sure me or Pa will bring yer home. He's probably nothing to worry about otherwise why would the Miltons let him work for them? Maybe he's just simple."

Jack's attempt at making May feel more at ease about this man didn't work, but she was relieved that there would always be someone to bring her home.

Placing the rug over May's legs, Jack told May how he had been to Squire Hamilton's house on hearing that he was looking for gardeners to undertake a huge landscaping project that he was going to embark on. May was thrilled that if he should be employed at the Hamilton house estate, he wouldn't have to leave Ashley Green.

"Oh Jack, that's wonderful news, I was so worried that you would have to work far away again, I don't think the Milton's can afford to employ anyone just yet. Oh, Jack, you're so good to me, I couldn't bare it if you had to leave. Jack took his eyes off the road and turned to face May, looking into her deep olive-green eyes.

"May, my love, I am gonna do my very best to make you happy. I will always be here for you, to protect and care for you my sweet, beautiful May."

Putting her hand through the crook of Jack's arm, May was glad of the darkness, which hid her blushing cheeks.

CHAPTER NINE

Quinton Kingsley had been welcomed with opened arms into the grand mansion of Squire Cedric Hamilton, who had found it difficult to believe that he was the son of the late Jeremiah, whom he had known for many years. He remembered Quinton as a smartly attired young boy playing on the grounds of his estate with his own two sons many years ago. Sons, who had now abandoned him, for a new life in America, their correspondence diminishing slowly over the years. Cedric, who was now in his twilight years, had sadly resigned to the fact that he would probably never see his sons again.

The Hamilton mansion stood at the end of a wide sweeping driveway behind towering decorative iron gates and a surrounding high wall. Its extensive grounds had been left unattended for many years and were desperately in need of attention. Only a small area immediately surrounding the house had been partially maintained, with a small regularly, mowed lawn and flower beds, which in the summer months displayed brightly coloured chrysanthemums, tall blue and purple delphiniums, dainty asters, and sweetly perfumed rose bushes. Almost two-thirds of the house was not in use anymore, with huge white dust sheets covering each unique piece of antique furniture and window shutters remaining permanently closed. The staff was now down to a minimum, and like Jeremiah, Cedric had kept his same faithful butler for almost five decades. Wilkinson had, over the years, become more like a friend and companion to his employer.

Cedric and Quinton were seated around the Queen Anne oval walnut dining table. Cook was euphoric; it had been a long time since Hamilton House had received any guests and she'd had to prepare a lavish table spread. She was elated that Quinton Kingsley had taken the trouble to thank and compliment her cooking personally. The praise which Betty had received inspired her to prepare some of the old family favourites. It had been years since anyone had complimented her cooking and it had given her a renewed enthusiasm. Quinton had not yet mentioned anything about his father's will, or the business of the Huntley woman in any of his conversations with Cedric. He was biding his time for an appropriate moment, knowing that Cedric was enjoying having company and someone other than Wilkinson to converse with; he had said to himself that it was like having one of his sons back home again. Not being sure if Cedric was eccentric, or just in the early stages of senility, Quinton was taking full advantage of his generous hospitality and the fact that he was now being viewed and treated more like a family member than a mere guest.

"Quinton my dear boy, have some more venison,"

invited Cedric as he lifted the solid silver dome which covered the huge platter of meat. "Can't indulge too much myself these days you know, *doctor's orders*, gout and all that." His hearty laugh echoed around the immense dining room.

"Well, I hate to see such exquisite food go to waste," said Quinton, piling the venison onto his already full plate. "I must say, Uncle Cedric, I believe your cook is a damn sight better than my, Mrs Booth, back in London! You're a jolly fortunate fellow," declared Quinton, as he pushed as much food as possible onto his fork.

"Yes, I must agree with you on that, young Quinton, her cooking is first class, she has served me very well over the years."

Elsie opened the double oak doors, entering with a large tray on which was a steaming hot plum crumble and a jug of creamed custard, to the delight of Quinton. Elsie Summerfield, who was in her early forties had been employed on the Hamilton estate for the past five years, ever since becoming a widow. She lived in Ashley Green with two of her four children and was employed as a maid, but was put upon to do many other duties due to the staff shortage, as well as assisting Betty downstairs in the kitchen.

"That is a delight to my eyes Elsie, one of my very favourite desserts," roared Cedric, his eyes lighting up like a small child on viewing the dish which Elsie placed on the table.

"Just leave it to us, my dear, we can serve ourselves

can't we, Quinton," he voiced, as Elsie was about to dish up the desert. "You get yourself off home now Elsie, before it gets too late."

"Thank you, Sir," replied Elsie, grateful for her employer's thoughtfulness. All conversation came to a halt as Cedric and Quinton devoured a large bowl full of Betty's scrumptious plum crumble. Quinton was in his element.

"Have some more Quinton," implored Cedric, "It's a damn tasty crumble I say, Betty has excelled herself today."

"You're most generous Uncle Cedric, but I must save a little room to breath," replied Quinton, patting his bulging stomach.

"Then, I suggest that we retire to the library for coffee. I've got a couple of plans that I'd like to show you. I'd appreciate your advice Quinton, you being a young man of the world and all that."

Quinton was intrigued and followed Cedric through the panelled doors into the grand library, where two winged brown leather chairs stood on either side of the blazing fireplace. Leaded glass door cupboards covered the entire side of the opposite wall, each one filled with a multitude of leather-bound books. A huge leather-topped, mahogany pedestal desk took centre place in the room, standing on a huge luxurious rectangular blue and turquoise Persian rug. A silver coffee service had already been left on a small occasional table, and as Quinton eased himself into the armchair, Cedric spread out a large rolled-up plan onto the desk.

"Quinton, old chap, come and take a look at my new little venture that I'm considering embarking on. I'm seriously considering landscaping the grounds. I've had these plans drawn up by a local gardener, he's not quite your *Lancelot Brown*, but he does appear to be very capable!" Cedric roared with laughter at his little joke, turning his drooping cheeks bright red.

"Ahh, you're referring to Mr 'Capability' Brown no doubt," said Quinton, as he strode over to the desk. "He was a jolly fine landscape gardener; I've had the fortune to stroll in many of his superb designs."

Quinton was becoming bored with his host, and looking at gardening plans was not at all what he felt like doing. He poured out two cups of the strong black coffee, hoping that it would shift the drowsiness that had overcome him after consuming such a large meal. Placing Cedric's coffee down on the desk next to the plan, Quinton hovered over his shoulder attempting to show interest and trying to hold back his yawns.

"Well Cedric, that looks truly remarkable. When do you intend to commence with your project?" inquired Quinton.

"Got a fine young man from Ashley Green....good strong lad, eager to prove himself. Yes, had a chat with him just the other day and I've offered him a job on the project just as soon as it is up and running."

Quinton thought that this might be the ideal time

to open the subject that he'd been holding off since arriving at the Hamilton estate.

"*Ashley Green!*" he declared loudly, making Cedric look up from his plans with a start, "I do believe that is where my dear father owned a cottage, am I right Uncle Cedric?"

"Stuff and nonsense!" blurted out Cedric, turning puce with anger. "He was merely paying the rent on the cottage, and I'll have you know, he owes me six years rent, which no doubt I will never see. He has my soft heart and my appreciation of a beautiful woman to thank for my oversight on that matter. Such a shame. Such

a tragedy. Burnt alive while she slept. A delicate flower cut down in the midst of life. A golden-haired angel taken from this world too early! Yes, indeed Emma Huntley was as fair as the summer sunshine." Cedric slumped into the chair, clearly distressed and upset, his sunken eyes shining with un-shed tears. Quinton handed him his coffee.

"Drink your coffee Uncle, you've obviously taken this woman's death very badly....tell me ....that's if you can bear to, did she have any children," he asked slyly.

Cedric glared straight ahead as he sipped his coffee, suddenly realising that Quinton Kingsley was not, as he had thought up to this moment, unlike his cheating lying rogue of a father. Why after all these years had Quinton decided to visit him, he must have been through all of his father's documents by now and he must be aware that Emma Huntley was mothering his father's illegitimate daughter. What was this sneaky man up to? He was definitely sniffing for something. If I can't even trust my own sons anymore, I certainly can't trust the offspring of Jeremiah Kingsley he thought. Fed up with having everyone take advantage of him all of his life, due to his kind and trusting disposition, Cedric was not going to allow this conniving stranger, because, basically that's what he was, to spend one more minute under his roof or on his land.

"Quinton Kingsley, kindly take your belongings and remove yourself from my home, *immediately*! I was a damn fool to even think that you travelled all this way because you were concerned for me. As much as I don't approve of speaking ill of the deceased, you are an exact copy of your late father, an utter disgrace to mankind, a scrounging, self-centred low life. Now, I bid you goodbye."

Quinton was dumbstruck; this was not the response he had expected. Had Cedric really seen through his motives, or was this aged man just slightly mad, he had thought?

"Uncle, come and sit down next to the fire," he insisted, coaxing Cedric from behind his desk. "You're clearly still suffering from this recent traumatic incident."

"Get off me boy!" he boomed. "I know your game, and I'm not the fool that you take me for."

"Believe me, Uncle Cedric, you are making a huge mistake here. Give me a chance to explain myself, and if you still feel the same, then I will leave straight away."

Cedric viewed him through squinted eyes, not wishing to hear what he knew would be a string of lies, but, if that's what it took to make him leave, he would grin and bear it. He didn't want any trouble and doubted that together, he and Wilkinson were strong enough to physically remove him themselves.

"Go ahead," sighed Cedric, "say your piece and make it quick."

Quinton had, for the last five minutes been trying to contrive a feasible story to tell Cedric, and hoped that what he was about to say would be convincing.

"Well, Uncle," he began.

"Do not call me Uncle, I am Squire Hamilton to you, you insolent young pup," declared Cedric angrily, his eyes full of contempt. Quinton realised that he was in for a difficult time. It seemed that Cedric had already made up his mind, without even hearing him out. Quinton swallowed hard, his mouth was dry, his palms sweating, and his shirt collar seemed to be shrinking around his wide neck. He felt uncomfortable and annoyed with himself for the way that he had handled this delicate matter. He hadn't known that Cedric had a soft spot for Emma Huntley. Ridiculous old flirt, he thought.

"I admit, it's true, that I knew of the late Emma Huntley, but I promise you, Uncle...I mean Sir, I knew nothing of her tragic death. I happened to have come across some documents while sorting through Father's desk, which made for a most enlightening read. Of course, I always knew of the existence of Father's illegitimate child, dear Mother had told me. *Poor Mama.* So I thought I would travel up to Cheshire, firstly to pay my respects to you, because I know what a good friend you were to my dear father; he always thought very highly of you, and secondly, I was curious to see my half-sibling, since I no longer have any close remaining blood relatives. I thought perhaps I might be able to help her, and her mother, financially, since my father's regular payments have now of course ceased. So you see Unc...Sir, you have misjudged me.

"Stop there," commanded Cedric, raising his hand, "I have heard enough, why didn't you just continue with the regular payments after your father passed away.....you are up to no good, I can sense it. There are rumours in Ashley Green that someone deliberately set fire to the cottage, knowing that they were inside....was that your doing...it's the sort of thing that your father would stoop to."

Quinton walked towards the door, annoyed that he had failed to convince Cedric, and even more angry that he wouldn't be able to fall into bed and sleep the night, but have to begin another arduous journey at such a late hour. Holding on to the shiny brass door handle, he turned around to face Cedric. "I will take my leave of you now Sir, you have obviously seen fit to condemn an innocent man, and it's of no wonder that your sons have abandoned you. After all, who in their right mind would wish to spend time with a soured old pompous blackguard like yourself?" Quinton's clenched fists were itching to knock the living daylights out of Cedric, but even he wouldn't attack such an old man. He had to contain his temper, at least, until he had left the house and then, with a bit of luck, he might be able to sniff out those Haines brothers and put them in their place. Oh what a damn mess, he thought to himself.

"I do believe that you have just described yourself, Quinton, now go before I get my staff to throw you out."

Cedric was amused; he knew he was nothing of what Quinton had just accused him of being. They were merely words, words from the mouth of a no-good scoundrel. Cedric was just angry that he hadn't seen through his scheming house guest when he had first shown up.

CHAPTER TEN

The sun had already set, and it was fast becoming dark as Quinton marched out of the wide shingled entrance of Hamilton House. He was pleased that he had asked Gascoigne to pack lightly, at least he only had a small valise to carry on his journey, he thought. There was no sign at all of any horse carts on the road that he could flag down for a lift, not a soul in sight. He was surrounded by fields and distant trees, which were giving the appearance of huge mountains in the fading light. He had to try and make it to Boxwell before he was totally overwhelmed by darkness. The moon was hidden behind a thick blanket of cloud, as a continuous steady downpour of sleet began to fall, soaking Quinton for the second time that week. Shivering, he pulled his jacket collar tightly up around his neck, bowed his head, and strode on. Half an hour later he found himself in the hamlet of Ashley Green. A handful of cottages in two neat rows on either side of the bumpy winding track was a welcoming sight to Quinton, as tiny glimmers of light shone from the miniature cottage windows. He noticed the burnt-out shell of what must have been Emma Huntley's home. Stopping for a brief moment, he wondered if his illegitimate half-sister was somewhere nearby. Cedric had only mentioned that Emma had died in the fire. Why hadn't he asked that Elsie woman, about her, she would have known; and where were those damn brothers hiding. Yet again Quinton could feel every muscle in his body tensing up as he clenched his fists.

Mary Weaver was looking out from a slight gap in her curtains, a new habit of hers since the night of the fire. Catching sight of Quinton as he walked past her cottage, she became instantly alarmed. It was most unusual to spot a stranger in the hamlet, especially at this time of night.

"Jack, come and look!" she said anxiously.

Jack had brought some firewood to the cottage for them, one of the many items which he showed up with most evenings as an excuse to spend time with May. As he peered out of the window, Cedric had already walked past, leaving Jack with just a back view of him.

"I don't know who that is, doesn't look familiar to me," said Jack, as he strained his eyes. "Might just go and catch up with him, check him out. I don't like the thought of strangers lurking around the hamlet, not after...well, I don't like it." Jack was already through the door and pulling on his cap, behind Quinton.

"Excuse me!" he called, "Have you lost your way, Sir?"

Turning around, Quinton smiled in appreciation of a voice on this dismal night.

"Ahh, young man, I can't tell you how pleased I

am to find someone out on this miserable evening. I'm making my way to Boxwell, and require a room for the night. Am I heading in the right direction, by chance?" enquired Quinton, pulling a handkerchief from his pocket to wipe his wet face. Jack eyed him suspiciously, something was not right here, he thought. What was an expensively dressed, well-spoken gentleman doing roaming around these parts alone and by foot on such a foul evening, something was definitely amiss here. Jack was in a quandary as to what he should do. Should he help him reach his destination safely? But was this stranger to be trusted, he thought. Jack had a very uneasy feeling about this man and decided that he should invite him into his cottage to see what his father could make of him.

"Would yer like to come in and dry off a bit before you continue on yer way, I live just over there in that cottage with me pa," said Jack pointing to his home.

"Young man, that would be greatly appreciated," replied Quinton, thinking that this would be his ideal opportunity to try and sniff out some valuable information. Jack led him to his cottage, where Bart, who was snoring gently as he dozed in the armchair in front of the fire, awoke suddenly on hearing Quinton's unfamiliar voice.

"Come in Mr...Mr....sorry, I didn't catch your name," said Jack, knowing that this stranger hadn't yet introduced himself.

"My name is Edward, Edward Berry," lied Quinton.

"Well, I'm Jack, Jack Turrell, and this is my pa, Bart." Bart stood up, still wondering why Jack had invited this stranger into their home.

"How do," uttered Bart, who was now standing face to face with Quinton, the cottage seeming very cramped now as all three stood in the tight living area.

"Mr Berry is on his way to Boxwell Pa, but wasn't too sure if he was heading in the right direction, and since it's such a raw night, I invited him in to dry off a bit."

"Well yer best take off that jacket then," suggested Bart, not at all pleased with Jack for bringing him home.

Jack hung Quinton's soaked jacket onto the back of a chair, placing it in front of the fireplace. "You best take a seat then, while Jack fetches you a hot drink. Now tell me, what are yer doing wandering around up here?"

Sitting on a small wooden chair, which felt like it would give way beneath him at any moment, Quinton again found himself being questioned, only this time, he thought, by a common country peasant, to who he didn't believe he had to justify his actions.

"Well, to cut a long story short, old chap, I've been a house guest up at the Squire Hamilton's estate, but today I received word that I'm urgently needed back in London, as my dear wife has been taken dangerously ill. I intended to leave tomorrow at first light, but couldn't stop worrying about my beloved Daphne, and knowing that I wouldn't catch a wink of sleep, I decided to leave immediately. Oh dear, poor sweet Daphne. I do hope she will make it through the night." Quinton's sadness had been inspired by his miserable low mood, but it seemed to have worked. He could see the look of concern in Bart's eyes as he told his sad story. Jack returned with three mugs of hot cocoa, he had heard every word that Quinton had said, but unlike his pa, he wasn't so trusting of this man. His story made no sense. Surely Hamilton would have arranged for a carriage to take his guest to the railway station in Chester, and it made no sense for Quinton to be looking for an inn for the night, how would that bring him to his wife's side any quicker, he thought?

There was an uncomfortable atmosphere as the three men sat in silence with their mugs of cocoa; the rising steam from Quinton's drying jacket filled the room.

"Damn shame about that fire in the cottage nearby, tragic by all accounts. Squire Hamilton told me that a poor young woman lost her life. Damn shame. Did the poor woman have a family?"

Jack sent his pa a warning look, he didn't trust or believe this man, so decided to play him at his own game.

"No, fortunately, she lived alone," replied Jack, noticing immediately a wave of shock on his face. Quinton began to feel claustrophobic, and uncomfortable. He knew that Jack was telling lies and that he wasn't going to extract any useful information from him. Nothing so far had been successful since he'd arrived in Cheshire and he was beginning to regret ever coming all this way, as a sudden pang of homesickness suddenly swamped him.

"I'll bid you both farewell, you have been most kind, but I won't impose on you any further. Thank you for your assistance, now if you would be so kind as to point me in the right direction, I won't take up any more of your time," expressed Quinton, as he stood up retrieving his jacket from the back of the chair.

The kitchen table in the Milton's kitchen was covered in half-completed dresses, threads of every hue and tiny beads and sequins as Sarah and May worked extra hard trying to finish the beautiful garments before market day. Many of the wealthier women were now buying Sarah's handmade dresses, as they were so finely sewn and each one was unique. This time of year saw many an evening soiree being held, and Sarah would quite often sell her work to one of the buyers who owned ladies' dress shops, all the way from Chester.

"If only I could afford a sewing machine," sighed Sarah, rubbing her strained eyes, as the light was quickly fading, "I could turn out these dresses so much quicker. I could make a proper business of it."

"You never know," said May, optimistically, "if we work extra hours at this time of year, you may well be able to soon purchase one. Goodness, it's time I was leaving, Mr Turrell or Jack will be here shortly. Jenny and baby Adam are having such a long afternoon nap, I've barely seen Jenny today, and I *have* missed our little chats."

"*Little*," laughed Sarah, "that child doesn't know little chats. As much as I love her, it's nice to have a bit of peace occasionally, and talking of love, I've noticed how your eyes get a twinkle in them whenever Jack is mentioned....just reminds me of myself when I first started walking out with Stan...seems like a lifetime ago; so much has happened since then."

As Sarah's sewing ceased as she sat reminiscing on past years, May could feel her cheeks begin to blush, could everyone detect her feelings for Jack, she thought? May quickly collected her basket which Sarah had already generously filled to the top. After putting on her bonnet, wrapping her shawl around her shoulders, and saying goodbye to Sarah, she rushed out of the door and hurried across the yard.

A light dusting of snow had fallen during the afternoon. The sun had been swallowed up by thick dreary clouds and the coldness of the outside air caused May to instantly shiver as she glanced around, hoping to see Jack. Standing on the roadside, her mind wandered to what Sarah had just said about her eyes twinkling when Jack was mentioned; yes, she did love Jack and was quite sure that his feelings for her were the same. Lost in her thoughts, she failed to hear or see Bill, as, like a wild animal stalking its prey, he quietly sneaked up behind her. His stinking hand covered her mouth and most of her small face, as his arms enclosed around her slight body, nearly squeezing the life from her as he lifted her body off the ground and ran back to his filthy den. May's heartbeat pounded. She was unable to breathe. Feeling so small and vulnerable in the clutches of this evil, foul-smelling monster, she had never in all her life been so petrified. In a state of sheer panic, she was terror-stricken as to what he was intending for her. Inside the dark and musty store room, the stench of the place hit May, making her feel immediately nauseous. Throwing her down onto a bail of hay, Bill, at last, removed his offensive hand from May's face, only to replace it with a piece of dirty, rough sacking, tying it tightly around her mouth, as Tom sat motionless and silent. After tying her feet, and her hands behind her back, he left. As her eyes adjusted to the darkness, she caught sight of Tom, who could do nothing but glare at her, sending shivers down May's spine.

Hearing the sound of the cart wheels upon the adjacent road, May silently prayed that Jack or Mr

Turrell would come to her aid.

It was Bart Turrell who had arrived to take May back to Ashley Green. Stopping just inside the farm entrance, thinking that May would soon show up, he noticed Bill heading towards him. He walked right up to the side of the cart, keeping eye contact with Bart the whole time. Bart, who wasn't one to judge people by their appearance couldn't help thinking how rough and unscrupulous Bill looked, and the thought of May working anywhere near this unsavoury-looking man, made Bart think that it wasn't such a good idea, after all; he would have a word with Mary when they arrived home. He knew that Emma would be very uneasy about this arrangement if she were alive.

"Yer looking for yer girl, Mister?" asked Bill, staring up at Bart, "only she went back inside ter wait, think she were cold... I would offer ter go an' fetch 'er, but I got a job ter do, Mister."

Bart climbed down from the cart, patting his horse reassuringly, and began to make his way across the snowy yard, thanking Bill for his help. The heavy blow that came down violently upon the back of Bart's head sent him falling to the ground, as he was immediately knocked unconscious. Hurling the heavy piece of wooden post into the hedge, Bill dragged Bart out of view to behind the small scrap heap. Within five minutes, Bill was jubilantly driving Bart's horse and cart as fast as it would gallop, with May and Tom thrown in the back like two sacks of coal.

CHAPTER ELEVEN

Jenny had woken up from her long afternoon nap and tiptoed into her parent's room, where baby Adam lay sleeping in his crib. Gently stroking his little chubby cheek, just as she had so often seen her mother do, she couldn't wait for the day when he would be able to play out in the yard with her; he wasn't really like a proper brother, she thought, as all he did was sleep, cry and have Ma's special milk.

Suddenly noticing, through the window, that the surrounding fields had all turned to white, Jenny was over-excited at seeing the first winter snow, even if it was only just a light dusting. Leaving the side of Adam's crib she rushed to the window. Rubbing the misty window pane with her little hand, her eyes were distracted from the snowy view to the goings on in the yard. Her young eyes were shocked; she couldn't believe what was happening. No sound escaped from her opened mouth, her dainty bare feet were stuck to the icy cold floorboards, and the inside of her tummy felt as if someone had tied a rope tightly around her. As Adam began to cry, waving his little arms around and kicking off his blanket, the long-awaited scream flew out of Jenny's mouth. A loud piercing scream, which reached every corner of the house; a scream which brought Sarah sprinting up the narrow staircase, two at a time, with a hundred terrible thoughts simultaneously spinning through her head. Even Stan, who was making his way back down to the house from one of the top fields, heard Jenny's howl.

When Sarah reached her bedroom, she found Jenny standing in a small puddle, the tears pouring from her bright startled eyes as her whole body shook from her heavy sobs. Sarah quickly swept her up into her arms, holding her close to her chest. Jenny was still unable to talk when Stan arrived in the bedroom, asking her what was wrong. In a state of panic, she was struggling to breathe. Stan picked up Adam in his arms, in the hope that, at least, he would stop his crying.

"Th...th...th...th...monster!" she suddenly shouted.

Stan and Sarah's eyes met, they were both having the same thoughts.

"She's been having a nightmare, poor love," voiced Stan, sympathetically as he rocked Adam, whose cries of hunger were increasing. "Come to yer pa, so Ma can feed Adam. We'll go downstairs and raid the larder," said Stan, trying to entice Jenny into his open arms. Sarah quickly dressed her in some clean dry clothes, and put the now, red-faced and angry baby on her breast. Stan carried Jenny down to the kitchen and sat her on a chair, while he went to look for something to cheer her up. He knew how scared Jenny was of Bill, but this was the first time that she'd had a nightmare about him; this was the final straw, he thought, tomorrow he would send him on his way, even if he had to take him and his brother himself. He'd had enough of that pair on his farm, terrifying his family.

"Strawberry jam on toasted bread, how does that sound," tempted Stan. Jenny nodded. She had calmed down a bit now, but her young mind was confused, she was so sure that she had witnessed Bill strike May's friend, she'd seen him throwing May onto his cart; maybe he had hit her too, maybe she was dead and he was taking her away. It wasn't a nightmare, she wasn't even in her bed, and she did see it, out of the window.

"Pa! Pa! Quick, it wasn't a nightmare, Pa. May's friend is out in the yard, Pa!"

Stan returned quickly from the larder, pot of jam in one hand, and half a loaf in the other.

"Jenny my love, nightmares can often seem so real, that you think they are true, anyway, tomorrow I'm sending the monster and his brother away for good, and then we'll all be happy again, won't we."

"He's already gone, and he took May with him, and May's friend is dead in the yard, Pa! Honestly," sobbed Jenny, as tears began to roll down her cheeks again. Stan sighed,

"Alright then, I guess I'm not gonna get any peace 'til I've taken a look out in the yard, am I?" Taking his coat and hat from the hook on the back of the door, Stan bent and gave Jenny a reassuring hug and ruffled her curls,

"yer ma should be downstairs soon, or should we wait for her before I go outside?"

"No Pa, I'll be fine. *Hurry Pa!*"

Stan walked to the store room, but there was no sign of Bill, who would normally be hanging around at this time of night, waiting for his and Tom's evening meal. He knocked hard on the storeroom door but didn't have to wait, as the door slowly swung open. The stench of decay and rot hit Stan, making him take a step backwards. It was pitch black and Stan couldn't see a thing.

"Bill! Tom!" he yelled. There was no reply. Stan felt uneasy, something was not right. Stan quickly crossed the yard, returning to the kitchen where grabbed the oil lamp and acknowledged Sarah who was sitting cuddling Jenny. He was gone again before Sarah had a chance to talk. This time as Stan walked across the yard, he could hear the sound of faint moaning coming from near the pile of broken and rusted old tools. Holding the lamp up high as he made his way towards the sound, he was beginning to realise that in fact, poor Jenny must have witnessed something horrendous. What of poor May, he thought, oh, Dear God, this was terrible, that poor young girl. Bart was struggling to stand up as he rubbed the back of his painful head.

"Mr Turrell," called Stan, as he neared him, "hold on. Let me help you." Bart was feeling dizzy as he stood up with the help of Stan. Struggling to support Bart's walk across the yard to the house wasn't an easy task for Stan, who cursed his disability under his breath. As they walked past the water pump, Stan broke off a hanging icicle; he knew that Sarah would suggest a cold pack on Mr Turrell's wounded head.

Inside the kitchen, Stan couldn't fail to notice the strain showing on his poor wife's face.

"Who would do such a terrible thing," she cried, as she inspected the back of Bart's head, while he sat on the settle, now feeling a little less dizzy. A large swelling was protruding from Bart's head, but Sarah thought it probably looked worse than it was. Wrapping the icicle in a piece of cloth, she urged Bart to hold it on his head for a while.

"Where's May?" Bart asked, realising that she was nowhere to be seen and remembering what Bill had told him. The sudden silence which fell in the kitchen was broken by the sound of Jenny's sobs.

"Jenny said that Bill took her in the back of your cart," declared Stan. "We thought she'd just had a nightmare and didn't believe her at first."

"Who is this Bill fellow?" asked Bart anxiously, attempting to get to his feet. Stan's face was etched with worry lines.

"Oh, Mr Turrell,"

"Please, call me Bart," he said, rubbing the back of his neck nervously.

"He and his brother came to us a few weeks back, they'd been robbed, or so they said, but I'm beginning to wonder. They were in a bad way, especially Tom. They had been in some barn fire and were injured, so with no money and being sick, I was stupid enough to allow them to live in the store room in return for some odd jobs around the farm. Oh God, what have I done? I had my doubts about those two from the moment they turned up. I've put my family in danger, and now it looks like they've disappeared with poor, sweet, young May. What could they possibly want with her?"

Bart's face turned a shade of grey, he had no idea where they had taken May, and he felt riddled with guilt, he should have been more like a Father to May, and checked this place out before she started working here, he thought. His head was throbbing and he couldn't think straight; too many strange things had happened in this area lately. Bart had been back and forth to the market, passing through Boxwell and the surrounding local areas, and he'd seen no sign of a barn fire, in fact, the only fire that had been spoken about recently was the one in Ashley Green. Those two vagabonds must have been the culprits, and now they had poor May in their evil clutches. Bart felt useless and sick with worry.

"I must go in search of May, they couldn't have got far, surely."

Stan was feeling guilty, bad luck seemed to follow him. Sarah, noticing that all too familiar depressed look on his face knew she had to reassure him quickly before he was again overtaken by the dark shadow of gloominess. She wouldn't be able to cope with another period like that.

"We have to alert the police, as quickly as we can," stated Sarah. "Let's pray that dear May has not been harmed in any way, that poor sweet child, she must be so scared," Sarah spoke quietly, hoping to protect Jenny's ears, but Jenny's imagination had already been working hard, as she continued to cry in hopelessness, the look of fear showing on her young face.

Stan had already gone out to the stable and was hitching his horse to the cart. He was determined to do all that was humanly possible to try and rescue May, and see Bill and Tom turned over to the law.

"Come on Mr Tur...Bart, I've got the horse ready, there's no time to spare, let's go and inform the constable in Boxwell, "stated Stan urgently.

Within two minutes, they were on the dark track with only the dim light from the diminutive oil lamp to guide them. The snow was no longer falling, but as the temperature plummeted to well below zero, the frozen ground made for a treacherous ride.

By the time they arrived in Boxwell, both Stan and Bart were sure that the fire and the death of Emma were the work of Bill and Tom.

Not since the death of Emma had Mary Weaver's tiny cottage seen such gloomy faces, as Mary, Bart, and Jack sat in silence, each one with their own thoughts and each one having a feeling of melancholy. The constable at Boxwell, although taking all the details down and sounding concerned, informed Bart and Stan that with such dire weather conditions and with it being so late, there would be no search until daylight tomorrow, and by that time they would probably be in another county, and no longer on his patch. Stan had driven Bart back to Ashley Green and promised to return at first light, when Bart, Jack, and Stan intended to form their own search party. Sarah couldn't get the image out of her mind, which Jenny had tearfully described to her, of poor May laying in the back of the cart. She must be terrified and feeling so alone and freezing cold, she thought, as fresh tears fell from her already sore eyes. If only I could turn back the hands of time, she wished.

CHAPTER TWELVE

Bill reached the dilapidated barn which he and Tom had spent the night in after the fire, it was as far as he could travel on such a cold and dark night, which threatened more snowfall. Bart's horse had also refused to move more than a slow trot, no matter how hard Bill cruelly tugged on the reins. The barn made the Milton's store room look luxurious in comparison, but it would do for the night, he thought, and at least he had a basket of food to keep him amused through the bitter night. Bill possessed no gentle manner in the way that he wrenched May from out of the back of the cart. Grabbing her slender ankles, he gave one sharp tug, causing her to land in a heap on the snowy floor; the pain caused her to cry out through the tightness of the sacking gag, whereupon Bill's heavy hand came down hard upon her face.

"Keep yer bloody mouth shut if yer knows what's good for yer."

He left her on the floor while he carried Tom off the cart, making him stand up and giving him a stern warning that he had to walk around inside the barn to get his leg muscles strong again, otherwise he'd be left behind. Next, he led the horse into the barn, not bothering to release the tired animal from the heavy wooden cart, just in case they needed to make a quick getaway before daylight.

Lastly, he returned for May. Her body shook with fear and cold. She knew that these were the men who had set fire to her home and killed her ma. These were the two who she had witnessed that night rummaging through the remains of the cottage, and most likely, these were the men who intended to kill her. Why didn't they just get it over with, she thought, and let her be united with her dear ma in the Hereafter?

"Why don't yer untie 'er, Bill," suggested Tom, "just for a bit, so she can 'ave some grub, she ain't gonna escape with you sat there like some fierce guard dog, is she?"

"You bloody idiot Tom, we ain't wasting this precious grub on the likes of 'er, it'll be like frowing it away, and she ain't starving like us, is she."

"Ah, please Bill, she's just a scared kid, look at 'er, where's yer 'art."

"So now I've got two bloody girls 'ave I," groaned Bill, as he emptied half of May's food basket onto the ground, dribbling uncontrollably at the sight of it.

"We ain't gonna do away with 'er Bill, I ain't 'aving no murder on me conscience, Bill. We could just tell 'er ter say nuffing, and we'll tell bloody Kingsley that we finished 'er off. What d'yer reckon Bill?"

"Are yer bloody mad or what, if we wanna get paid, we as ter bloody well snuff 'er out...Like a little candle," he said, turning to look at May, with an icy grin on his face. "Now, let's 'ave some grub before we starve ter bloody death."

"I ain't eating nuffing till yer untie 'er. Just undo 'er 'ands an' mouth Bill, so she can eat," pleaded Tom defiantly.

Growling like a savage beast, Bill yanked the sacking roughly from around May's mouth, which had swollen from the effect of Bill's previous heavy-handed blow and then untied her hands. He grabbed a slab of cheese, and broke it in half, leaving his dirty fingerprints on each portion.

"If yer wanna feed 'er, then it comes out of your share."

Although having completely lost her appetite, May, accepted the chunk of cheese which Tom passed her, along with a piece of his share of bread. She noticed how bad his hands looked, and knew that they must be giving him a lot of pain. She realised that he was the kinder and the weaker of the two brothers. Felling a great sense of revulsion and anger, knowing that because of them she had lost her ma and her world had been turned upside down she knew that if she was going to have any hope of surviving this ordeal, then the only possible way would be to get on the right side of Tom and gain his support. As she reluctantly nibbled on the food, her thoughts went to Mr Turrell, she prayed that he was alright; she had heard his voice when she was in the store room and knew that Bill must have done something dreadful to him. She wondered if Jack and Mrs Weaver knew what had happened and if anyone was out looking for her. What about Sarah, she probably thought that she was safely home in Ashley Green. May was unable to stop the tears spilling from her eyes.

"What else is in the basket then," spluttered Bill, as bits of chewed-up food fell from his mouth as he spoke.

"A few apples an' carrots," announced Tom, "an' we got a few spuds, which need cooking."

"Well what yer bloody waiting for? Put 'em in the oven then," growled Bill sarcastically. "Just chuck us an apple."

Tom held out an apple for May. "Give mine to the horse," she said, trying to blink away her tears.

"Ahh, ain't that sweet, she cares about the dumb animal, I'm touched," sniggered Bill, helping himself to another apple. Tom eased himself up from where he was sitting, slowly walking over to the horse with a few carrots and two apples. He was a pitiful-looking man, thought May, as she watched him out of the corner of her eye, but at least he had feelings and showed that he was caring, unlike his awful brother.

"Poor 'orse needs ter eat or 'e ain't gonna move another step, Bill," said Tom, as he gently held the carrots to his mouth. Bill's eyes were firmly fixed on May, making her feel uncomfortable and anxious as she wondered what was going on in his mind. She dropped her gaze to the ground, as she nervously fiddled with the corner of her shawl, praying that someone would come and find her soon and that her captors might fall asleep; maybe then she could untie the painful, cutting ties on her ankles and escape.

Bill's beady eyes caught a glimpse of May's necklace. His hand stretched out suddenly as he grabbed her shawl, making May scream out in horror. May always wore her mother's pendant, with her gold ring attached to the chain, and kept it safely close to her heart and hidden under her clothing, but in all the commotion, a small part of the chain was now hanging out of the top of her dress.

"Give us that there necklace girl," Bill shouted, his eyes lighting up. May backed away with her hand placed on her neck. She could feel her heart pounding with fear.

"Don't touch me!" she screamed.

"Leave 'er alone Bill," pleaded Tom as he slowly sauntered back from feeding the horse, "she's just a kid, an' yer scaring 'er."

Bill was getting sick of his brother's pathetic ways, he had a good mind to dump both of them in the nearest canal, return to London and live off his reward, and enjoy life for a while, but he knew his ma would kill him, and she was the only one who could tell when he was lying. Letting out a loud groan, and giving Tom an evil look, he threw May's shawl down and held out his hand.

"Just give us that shiny thing round yer little neck, *Girly*, and I won't touch yer."

Reluctantly, May undid the clasp on the chain,

pulling it out gradually so that her ma's golden ring fell off the chain, remaining hidden beneath her dress. She handed the pendant and chain over to Bill, dropping it into the palm of his filthy hand. A sly grin moved over his face as he examined the piece of jewellery.

"This should fetch us three tickets back to London, with a bit to spare."

"What do yer wanna take 'er back ter London for Bill, let's just leave 'er 'ere an' go back 'ome ter Ma. Forget about that reward from Kingsley, we don't want 'is blood money, Bill. We can go back ter what we're best at."

"I ain't gonna kill 'er anymore Tom, I've bin finking, I got a plan for 'er. A pretty young maid like 'er is worth more alive than dead, understand what I'm saying, Tom."

May shuddered, she had to escape from these two, at least they weren't going to kill her, but if Bill's plan went ahead, she knew that she would be better off dead. If they were planning on taking her to London, then there would surely be an opportunity for her to give them the slip and escape from their evil clutches.

"In a couple of hours, we're gonna make tracks to Chester, so get some rest," Bill announced, in a sleepy voice. Within a minute he was snoring.

"Does your brother always eat himself to sleep," asked May.

"E's right greedy is Bill," whispered Tom cautiously, just in case Bill was listening with one ear.

"Did Mr Kingsley pay you to kill me then?" Looking at Bill, Tom nodded his head, "I never met 'im, me brovver did all the arrangements, I just tagged along." May sensed the sound of regret in his voice. "I didn't know 'e came up 'ere ter kill anyone."

"Your hands look very painful, let me bandage them for you," said May. Tom liked her, she was kind and caring. He didn't like to think of what Bill had in mind for her, if it was up to him, he would let her go free, and to hell with bloody Kingsley.

"Pass me one of those potatoes," said May.

"Yer can't eat raw spuds, me ma said they make yer really sick. If yer still 'ungry, there's a bit of bread left, Bill won't know, will 'e?"

"Oh no, I'm not going to eat it, I'm going to make a potion to put on your sore hands, it's very healing for burns; my aunty taught me."

Looking puzzled, Tom passed her a potato. Removing a hairpin from her hair, May began to scrape away at the potato until there was a small pile of wet pulp in front of her. Tearing off the end of her cotton petticoat to make a bandage, she gently began to spread the pulp over Tom's wounded hands and then bandaged each one with great care.

"There, they should soon feel much better." Thanking May, as he stood up and made his way over to the horse, Tom remembered seeing a thick rug in the cart and returned to give it to May, who hadn't been able to stop shivering, from fear as well as from cold, since they had arrived at the freezing barn.

"Put this over yerself, it might make yer feel a bit warmer, then yer can maybe 'ave a little nap. We're used ter kipping in the cold, me an' Bill."

May was reminded of Jack, and how he would always place the rug over her with such loving care, as she sat up next to him on the horse cart.

Taking the rug from Tom's hands, she was glad of its warmth on this bleak icy night, but she had no intention of going to sleep, hoping that before long, Tom would also be snoring like Bill, and she would be able to sneak out. Thankfully, Bill had fallen asleep before remembering to tie her hands again. In the meantime, with the thick rug covering her, she secretly set to work on untying the strips of rough sacking which bound her ankles together. Unable to sleep, Tom slumped against the side of the barn, staring into space, he was a very troubled young man, thought May. Bill continued snoring loudly, his mouth half open as dribble trickled out onto his filthy matted beard. Even though May had managed to release her ankles, she couldn't guarantee that Tom would keep quiet if she suddenly made a run for it, his loyalty to his bullying brother would undoubtedly force him to alert Bill. As the only measly candle melted away, May prayed for the daylight to return quickly.

CHAPTER THIRTEEN

"I can't bear to think about what that poor girl's going through, she's far too young to be 'aving to face such a terrible ordeal," exclaimed Mary, wiping a tear from under her eye. "Don't yer be coming back home without 'er now," she warned Jack and Bart Turrell, as they prepared to set out with Stan Milton, in search of May. Mary hadn't been able to sleep a wink through the night, she'd sat up in the hope that there would soon be a knock on the door, and by some small miracle, it would be May returning home. Thankfully, there had been no more snowfall through the night, but with sub-zero temperatures, and a strong northerly wind, the bleakness of the early morning did not invite anyone to leave the warmth of their firesides. Mary had packed the men off with a supply of boiled eggs, bread rolls and a handful of apples, praying for their journey to be successful.

As Stan Bart and Jack made their way along the frozen track, not sure in which direction to head first; Bill, Tom and May were halfway to Chester, having left the outskirts of Ashley Green an hour before sunrise. Bill had woken up in a fiery mood, dishing out a verbal explosion to Tom, condemning him for not tying May back up after he'd fallen asleep and accusing him of being taken in by her wily ways when he noticed the fresh bandages on his hands. All three of them were now sat upon the seat of the horse cart, with May squashed in the middle of the brothers, barely able to move. She had been left untied and given strict instructions that if anyone should ask, she was their sister. The penalty for disobeying Bill's orders, or doing anything to bring attention to herself, would be, as Bill had phrased it, a dip in the nearest river with a boulder fastened to her ankle. May sat quietly, feeling ill from the biting cold wind, lack of sleep and food, and the nauseating odour emanating from Bill and Tom.

"I doubt they got far last night, not unless they went by foot, I know my Chestnut, he refuses to budge come the evening, especially if he's not been fed properly." Bart was concerned about his old faithful horse but kept it to himself since the safety of dear May was, of course, the most pressing issue on all of their minds.

"I reckon they must have spent the night somewhere," stated Stan, "as little as I know Bill, I can vouch that he ate all the food which my wife had packed in the basket for May to take home with her, and then had to sleep it off. They probably left the area a short while ago, with the first daylight."

Bart was more worried that they had done something terrible to May, knowing that their mission was to end her life, he just prayed that perhaps they'd had a change of heart, but remembering that scoundrel, Bill, he felt his blood run as cold as the frozen snow.

"I think we should look in every possible place that they could've stayed in last night," suggested Jack, "maybe they abandoned May somewhere, in the hope that nobody would find her until it was too late."

The very thought made him feel physically sick, if they were too late, he would never forgive himself.

Bill left the Chester pawn broker's shop baring his brown stained and broken teeth in a triumphant smile. He was thrilled at the amount he'd persuaded the broker to give him and jubilant to have some money. The aged pawn- broker had watched him suspiciously through the blinded window, as he rejoined Tom and May, immediately feeling concerned for the worried-looking girl, who appeared out of place with her two dubious-looking companions. He had felt threatened by Bill's rude and aggressive manner, handing him twice as much as the silver necklace was worth. Placing it safely in a drawer, his instincts told him that something was not right. He would keep hold of it, just in case. Still looking through the window, he watched as the other man and the girl alighted from the cart. All three of them headed towards the railway station, which was directly opposite. The pawnbroker noticed how the man, who he had just served, had a tight hold on the girl's arm, just above her elbow. She stopped a couple of times, as if refusing to walk, constantly turning her head in every direction, as if she was searching for someone. He was quite sure he could see tears on her cheeks as he caught the last glimpse of her before the three of them disappeared into the crowds near the station entrance.

Bart, Jack and Stan had looked in every outbuilding, shed and barn that they had passed, but came nowhere nearer to any sign of May and the two brothers. Most of the farmers had been very obliging, allowing their premises to be searched, especially when they heard of what had happened to May, their genuine sympathy, and concern moving many more to join the search party.

"Let's take a look over there," said Bart, pointing to the remains of a run-down barn at the edge of an overgrown field.

"No one in their right mind would even risk entering that place, let alone spending a winter's night inside it," scolded Jack.

"Well then, we'd best have a look, those two brothers are definitely barmy enough to do just that," declared Stan, as he directed the horse around towards the barn.

"I'll take a quick look," said Jack, jumping down from the cart and pacing towards the ram-shackled barn. The sight that he was met with caused him to freeze in shock, as a wave of desperation and disappointment seemed to sweep through his very soul. Just knowing that May had spent a freezing cold night in such a bleak place, along with that pair of despicable crooks, stirred his emotions, making him long to be close to May and protect her. He'd left it too late, this should never have happened, he thought to himself angrily. Bart and Stan were soon behind him, wondering what was keeping him so long.

"Oh, Dear God!" declared Stan, catching sight of his wife's upturned basket and its few remaining items, strewn over the filthy floor along with half a dozen apple cores and potatoes which had been strangely picked at. Bart noticed the thick brown rug from his horse cart. May's pretty bonnet also lay abandoned on the ground.

"Looks like they left in a hurry," said Bart, in a deflated voice.

"Why don't we go to the Hamilton estate, Pa? If the Squire will see us, maybe he can shed some light on that Edward Berry, I'm positive that he's somehow behind all this."

Thinking the idea over for a couple of minutes, Bart decided that it might not be such a bad idea to investigate Edward Berry further. Since meeting him that night, Bart and Jack were both left with a nagging feeling that he had something to do with poor Emma's death. They set off to the Hamilton estate, filling Stan in on the way about the mysterious stranger that had turned up in the hamlet a few nights ago.

Bill dashed into a nearby apothecary, where he purchased a small bottle of laudanum. He intended to sit back and relax on the journey to London, it had been a gruelling few weeks, and he wanted to put it behind him. Being on guard constantly, in case May did anything stupid was hard work, so he'd decided to quieten her down a bit.

"How about we 'as a nice cuppa before our journey," Bill suggested, with a familiar smug-looking grin on his face, causing May to cringe. Inside the tea room, their presence prompted the existing patrons to consume their food and drinks hurriedly. The young waitress had never before had to serve such loathsome-looking customers. She felt sorry for May, noticing that she wasn't wearing a wedding band on her finger, she presumed that the two men were her brothers or close relatives. She looked a lot cleaner and classier than her companions. Serving them quickly with the three cups of tea they had ordered and a large piece of fruit cake for the one with the hideously scared face, she hoped they would not linger in the tea room.

Their revolting odour smelt worse than the river on a bad day. May watched anxiously as Bill poured some of the laudanum into her tea,

"Drink up girl, that'll make yer feel much better."

"I'm not drinking that!" declared May, emphatically, pushing the cup and saucer away from her, "*you're trying to poison me!*"

Bill's clenched fist slammed down heavily onto the small circular table causing the tea cups to rattle and causing an instant silence to fall in the tea room, as everyone looked to where they were seated. Under the table, Bill grabbed May's leg, squeezing it with his strong grip as he looked into her alarmed eyes, "just drink yer tea, there's a good girly, or you'll be *under* the next train that pulls in ter the station, instead of being on it. Do yer understand?"

On many occasions, Tom loathed his brother, but today, he felt nothing but pure hatred towards him. He knew all too well how it felt to be bullied by him and what it was like to be on the receiving end of his wrath. To think how over the years, he had tried to mirror his older brother, envious of the power he seemed to have over everyone, but it had suddenly dawned on him that he was nothing but a repugnant bully, with no feelings for anyone. He was an empty shell with no heart. Today he had decided that things were going to change, and for that to happen he would have to make a clean break away from Bill, and away from the hold that he had always held on him. He was no longer going to be Bill's weak little puppet at his beck and call. He would do his best to see that no harm came to this poor kid too, who had shown nothing but kindness to him, but he'd only be able to save her with the help from his ma, back in London.

As they left the tea room the drug soon took

effect on May, causing her to stumble and fall like a drunkard. Unable to stand, Bill, picked her up, carrying her in his arms as they waited on the platform for the arrival of their train.

"See what yer've done now Bill, why did yer make 'er drink that stuff, she weren't giving us any trouble."

"Just shut yer bloody face up, leave the real work ter those that know what they're doing, alright little brovver," cautioned Bill, his face red with anger. "Remember, I could 'ave left yer for dead weeks ago, but I took care of yer, didn't I?"

"Yeah, only ter save yer only bloody neck, an' cos Ma would kill yer if yer left me up 'ere."

"Is that the bloody thanks I get for caring 'bout yer, an' working like a bloody slave under old farmer Milton all day long, just ter keep yer safe till yer got better!"

Bill's angry, raised voice was attracting the attention of the small groups of people waiting on the platform.

"Just bloody leave me alone will yer, I've 'ad enough of yer, Bill. I wish I'd never come up 'ere with yer."

"Yeah, you an' me both!" yelled Bill, his temper getting the better of him as he lashed out with his boot, kicking Tom, and causing him to collide with a small group of women and children. The cries of the startled women along with the bawling children soon bought the station master hurrying towards them.

After checking that no damage had occurred, he

turned to Bill, "Is everything quite alright Sir, only you seem to be creating a bit of a commotion over here."

Not liking the look of Bill, he eyed him suspiciously. "Is the young Miss sick," he questioned, glancing at May in Bill's arms. Bill shuffled nervously from one foot to another.

"It's me, poor little sister, she's right poorly, an' me brovver 'ere is coming down with something too, 'appen that's why 'e fell over."

"Oh dear me," said the station master, straightening his cap, "I'll let you travel in your own special carriage then, after all, we don't want all the passengers to become sick, do we now." The station master antagonised Bill even more, if he didn't have this pathetic girl in his arms, he'd give this idiot a good beating, he thought, trying his best to stay calm. Ordering them to follow him, he led them to a carriage which inside was even worse than third class, with not even the basic comfort of any hard wooden slatted seats. Half of the small carriage was filled with a pile of coal, causing a permanent dirty, dust cloud to fill the air. Since they would be changing trains after a few stops, Bill obligingly went along with the arrangement, making a minimal fuss. His main aim was to get as far away from this place, and as soon as possible.

Cedric Hamilton had been more than pleased to

assist Bart, Jack, and Stan, telling them what a ruthless cad the alias Edward Berry was. On learning that his real identity was Quinton Kingsley, Bart and Jack immediately knew that the man they had allowed to set foot inside their cottage was May's half-brother. The situation immediately seemed to be more dangerous, and it was probably most likely that May was no longer in the area. Cedric gave Bart Quinton's address, warning them to all be on their guard and to tread carefully. He still couldn't believe how that sly fox had managed to fool him and abuse his hospitality. Asking them to keep him informed on any developments and wishing them success, he handed them a generous sum of money to cover the expense of their search, saying that it was the least he could do, being that his health didn't allow for him to join them. Just before they left, Cedric took Jack to one side, telling him that the gardening job was his if he was still interested and that he was hoping to commence the project in early spring. Accepting gratefully, Jack's euphoria was greatly marred by the nightmare of May's abduction.

CHAPTER FOURTEEN

Quinton strode into the Eagle Gentlemen's club making a beeline for his favourite leather balloon chair, tucked away in the corner. He was infuriated after returning home to find Gascoigne's letter of resignation, and even more irritated by the clear evidence that, before leaving he had rummaged through all of the private drawers in his desk. He would search him out, he thought to himself angrily, if it was the last thing he did. Gascoigne would get his comeuppance. After the lousy few days, he'd experienced in Cheshire, without a sniff of those damn Haines brothers, to return to London, only to find his trusty butler had deserted him had been the final straw to a disastrous week. To top it all, Mrs Booth had taken to her sick bed, and that stupid maid, Lizzie, didn't know the difference between a pie and a flan. The entire house was in need of a massive shake-up, but, thought Quinton, his most paramount mission was to visit Mr Fenwick, to inform him of the tragic news of the death of the Huntley women. Then he would dig out those useless scoundrels, who he thought, must be living back in the squalor of the East End by now.

Taking out his pocket watch, as he picked up a newspaper from the small leather topped table, he realised it was still too early to call in at Fenwick, Fenwick, and Montague. Feeling profoundly unsociable, he hid behind the outspread newspaper trying to block out all the political talk which filled the smoky room. He was already sick of hearing about the new American president-elect, Abraham Lincoln, and he hadn't even taken office yet. Why people were so intrigued with American politics, he just couldn't understand, especially when there was so much talk about a potential war, since this *Lincoln* was all in favour of abolishing slavery. With too many issues occupying his thoughts, Quinton found it impossible to settle. Outside, he welcomed the cold fresh air, hoping it would clear his head. A brisk walk around the park, he thought, before going to face that pompous Mr Fenwick, and then he would set about finding Bill Haines and that impudent Gascoigne.

Just around the corner from the park were the offices of Fenwick, Fenwick, and Montague in Chapel Street, situated on the ground floor of a lofty four-storey townhouse. Quinton looked at his pocket watch, as he pushed open the smart, dark blue front door, which, as usual, was unlocked. He stepped into the black and white square-tiled hallway. A large ornate brass-rimmed oval mirror hung from one wall opposite an overgrown aspidistra which was seated on a grand decorative porcelain pedestal One of the doors off the hallway opened slowly and Mr Fenwick's clerk appeared to greet him. A tall spindly pale-faced man with a protruding hooked nose and bushy sideburns. He recognised Quinton immediately from the few occasions when he had accompanied his father to Mr Fenwick's office when he was much younger.

"Good morning Mr Kingsley. I trust you are well. Do you wish to make an appointment to see Mr Fenwick?" Shocked that the clerk knew his name, Quinton replied,

"I was hoping to see, Mr Fenwick, this morning, if he's in his office, of course."

"Please wait here, Mr Kingsley, while I check Mr Fenwick's diary."

A couple of minutes later the clerk returned and ushered Quinton into Mr Fenwick's office.

"Good morning, Mr Kingsley, do come in and have a seat."

As the two gentlemen shook hands, George Fenwick couldn't help but notice how sweaty Quinton's palms were, on such a cold morning. "I must say, this is a most pleasant surprise, you have saved me yet another journey to your home. I have called no less than three times over the past two weeks. Undoubtedly, you are an extremely busy man."

"Yes," replied Quinton in a very sombre voice, "I've been in Cheshire, where I received the most devastating news of the demise of my poor unfortunate half-sister and her mother."

Quinton glanced down, unable to meet Mr Fenwick's eyes, which seemed to be boring into him.

"That is indeed tragic news, Mr Kingsley; you have my sincere condolences. Do you have the death certificates with you, so that we can proceed with the reading of your late father's will as soon as possible?"

Quinton didn't like how Mr Fenwick had reacted to his tragic news, his condolences had a ring of insincerity about them too.

He sighed heavily, "I did obtain the death certificates, but I have unfortunately been taken for a fool by my last butler, and in such a terrible time when I am struck down with such grief."

"I don't understand," replied Mr Fenwick, looking confused. "Are we talking about Gascoigne here?"

"The very same. That no-good rogue resigned; left me without giving any notice while I was out, and not before sifting through my private drawers and removing many official documents, including the death certificates. I cannot begin to think why he should want such documents, and furthermore, I have no idea where he is now residing."

"Oh dear, that is very unfortunate, very unfortunate indeed," mumbled Mr Fenwick, as he fiddled with his ink blotter. "I presume you have informed the police of this theft, Mr Kingsley."

"Indeed I have," he lied, "so now Mr Fenwick, am I right in assuming that we can now go ahead with the reading of my late father's will? After all, nearly nine months have passed since his death."

George Fenwick felt unsettled, he had never quite

taken to Jeremiah's son, didn't feel that he could trust him, and in this instant, didn't believe him.

"I'm afraid it's not as simple as that, Mr Kingsley. Due to the fact that both the deceased whom you have mentioned are beneficiaries of your father's estate, I will not be able to proceed until I have obtained copies of the death certificates."

Quinton was running out of patience. "However, I *am* able to release a small amount of your father's capital, which isn't tied up in his assets, if you wish, Mr Kingsley."

George Fenwick could see that this case was likely to drag on even longer. He intended to give it all his attention, the sooner it was closed, the better, he thought.

Quinton stood up abruptly to leave, holding out his hand to George, he said, "Well I'll leave it in your very capable hands, Mr Fenwick, I trust I will hear from you when you have sorted out my father's affairs, and yes, if you would transfer some funds into my bank, that would be most acceptable, until my birthright is finally released to me."

Quinton left the office without giving George the chance to answer him, leaving him thinking what a rude and spoilt man Jeremiah's only son had grown into. He was positive that there was something untoward going on in all this; it was just too much of a coincidence that both the Huntley women had died before the reading of Sir Jeremiah Kingsley's will. A reading, which Quinton had postponed more times than he could remember.

Quinton marched angrily down Chapel Street, making his way back home. His mind was in turmoil. There were too many loose ends, and he'd have to be careful, otherwise, the consequences could bring about his downfall. He wasn't an astute businessman like his father had been, in fact, he had never done a proper day's work in his life, and he didn't intend to start now. If his father had been foolish enough to leave that illegitimate peasant a handsome amount of his wealth, that's presuming she was still alive, then it didn't bear thinking about how his finances would be affected. He just hoped that Bill had successfully accomplished what he had set out to do.

As he turned the corner into Windsor Avenue, Gascoigne happened to be peering out of his window, checking the weather conditions. This was the first time that he had set eyes on Quinton since his resignation, and since moving into his cosy room on the second floor. A feeling of satisfaction overwhelmed him, knowing how annoyed Quinton must have felt on returning home from his travels to find he no longer had his trusty butler to vent all his anger on. Gascoigne was reminded of the documents that he had taken from Quinton's desk. Although he didn't intend to leave London until the spring arrived with the warmer weather, he would definitely take a journey to that dubious address in the East End to check out that *Bill* fellow, and try to find out his connection with Kingsley.

CHAPTER FIFTEEN

If there was one aspect Martha Haines disliked about her job, it was having to set out from home so early in the morning for the forty-five-minute journey, especially on such bitingly cold frosty days. With her shawl wrapped tightly around her head, she kept her eyes peeled for any passing carriages that she could hitch a ride on, to save her ageing legs. Her employers at the Eagle Gentlemen's club believed that Martha lived closer by, and in a more decent and respectable area than the slums of the East End. She had no choice but to lie, it was the only way she could secure a decent job. A job that she'd inherited from her younger sister, Edith, who, after the tragedy of her daughter's death nearly eighteen years ago, could no longer bring herself over the threshold of the club. Martha's life had been one long constant struggle against poverty and disease, but she had sworn a solemn oath to herself many years ago after her husband had left her, that she would never, as many of her neighbours had done, sell her body. She would rather starve.

As young children, she and Edith had dreamed of becoming actresses, spending many hours hanging around outside the theatres and often sneaking in to catch a glimpse of the performances. They had both mastered the ability to mimic the gentry, using these skills to their advantage. Martha was able to put on airs and graces and was proud of the way she could *'talk posh'* as she would put it. She used her skill, along with a string of alias names, to obtain various jobs. Working at the Eagle Gentlemen's club had become her favourite and most long-standing job. Previously, she had worked in many of the grand houses which had been converted into lawyers' and solicitors' offices. She remembered how, in days gone by, she would leave the children sleeping as she quietly left home in the early morning, clean the grand offices, taking pride in polishing the rich mahogany and rosewood furniture, and return home before the youngsters had woken. That was before she had lost her two dear beloved daughters to an outbreak of cholera. Dark days in the East End, which saw too many tiny pine coffins and left every single family in mourning. Their father had not had to endure the pain of watching his offspring fighting for their lives until their last breath had taken them. He'd left in search of a better life the previous year and never returned. No one had seen or heard from him, but Martha still believed that he was alive somewhere, probably in America, as he had often spoken to her of his desire to go gold panning in the hope of striking it rich. She doubted he would ever return to her though.

Eighteen years ago, when Edith worked at the Eagle Gentlemen's club, she would bring her daughter, Agnes, with her to help with the cleaning; it meant that the work could be done in half the time. Edith's husband, who wasn't in favour of his wife and only daughter working, helped run the family business, a small fleet of hand carts from which hot meat pies and mashed potatoes were sold. He earned enough, but Edith wanted to move up in the world, sick of living in an overcrowded and filthy tenement building, she dreamed of moving into a small terraced house, with a backyard, and its own privy.

It was on a day when Agnes had returned to the club to retrieve her forgotten bonnet that she bumped into Sir Jeremiah Kingsley. It was a day that Edith wished with all her heart that she could rewrite. From the moment that Jeremiah set eyes on Agnes, he was captivated by her youthful beauty. She was so gentle and graceful, with the most dainty and elegant figure that he had ever seen in a woman. Her coyness intrigued him, and from their first accidental meeting, he found himself thinking about her continuously. He couldn't erase her enchanting face from his mind, every time he closed his eyes, she was there. He found himself going to his club earlier every morning, in the hope of seeing her again, but when he did catch sight of her, she was never alone, but with who, Jeremiah could only presume, was her mother.

Edith became suspicious, wondering what his intentions were, and instructed Agnes to stay well clear of him. He was a sly-looking older man, who was out to satisfy his lusts, nothing but trouble, she had warned her. Jeremiah persuaded the porter, with a handsome tip, to pass on a note to Agnes, asking her to meet him in the nearby park, but although Agnes had been aware of the fact that Jeremiah had his eye on her and was slightly curious, she obeyed her mother and ignored the note. As disappointed as Jeremiah was, he didn't give up, and eventually, Agnes made a diversion to the park while on a shopping errand for her mother, more out of curiosity than anything else.

Over the next few months, Jeremiah plied Agnes with lavish gifts and trinkets, and whenever possible took her to expensive restaurants, and on a couple of occasions, he booked them into a hotel room, telling Agnes that he didn't want her to become ill from walking out in all weathers. In her naivety, she believed every word he said. She felt guilty betraying and lying to her parents, and on each secret meeting, intended to tell Jeremiah that it would be their last. He was besotted with her, and Agnes was revelling in all the attention and generosity that he was showering on her.

When Edith eventually realised what had been going on, it was too late. Agnes had fainted a couple of times, making Edith think that her daughter hadn't been getting enough nourishment, but when she started being sick every morning, Edith straight away recognised the symptoms. She was devastated, how could Agnes have been so stupid? How could she ruin her life like this, and shame the family, Edith thought, feeling a wave of panic rush through her at the thought of everybody finding out. Confiding in her husband, they decided that they would do their best to keep the whole sorry affair a secret, to save the shame and the embarrassment, and in the hope to secure a better future for their only child. Agnes was no longer permitted to leave the home, and Edith intended to forsake her job at the Eagle Gentlemen's club as soon as the baby was born. She also made some enquiries at the club, finding out that the cad who had ruined her daughter's life was married with a son. After finding the stash of expensive gifts which Jeremiah had given to Agnes, hidden in her cupboard, Edith was so enraged that she sought Jeremiah out and followed him home. As he walked up the few steps to his front door, she marched up behind him and violently shoved the small bag of gifts into his hands. She said nothing, but just stood staring into his startled-looking face, her furious, hateful look hit Jeremiah like the bite of a venomous viper. He left her standing there and like the coward he was, quickly scurried inside, closing the door on Edith.

The final three months before the birth, became three months of constant lies and excuses. Agnes was confined to bed with a mysterious ailment, which was possibly contagious, this was the lie Edith and her husband had told to anyone asking after their daughter. All three of them spent many nights in prayer, asking God to forgive their sins. Agnes was riddled with guilt as she witnessed her dear parents in turmoil, their faces permanently frowning and worried. She had ruined all of their lives with her foolish actions, and taken away their smiles and happiness.

It was mid-July when Agnes went into labour. After fifteen long hours of agony, she finally delivered a daughter. As she held the tiny infant in her arms, the guilt she had felt over the past months seemed to disappear. She felt nothing but pure love for her beautiful baby, a different kind of love from any other, which brought with it an instant surge of protection towards the small bundle of life. Edith became alarmed when after an hour had passed, there was still no sign of the afterbirth. In a state of sheer panic, she helped Agnes onto her feet, helping her walk around the room in the hope that this would help. A sudden gush of bright red blood, causing Agnes to pass out made Edith scream for help.

The doctor arrived half an hour later. Agnes had turned a ghostly white and the bleeding had not ceased. He shook his head in a look of hopelessness at this all too familiar sight. It wasn't the first time, and it wouldn't be the last that a young lass had lost her life from haemorrhaging after childbirth, he had gravely muttered.

The doctor gently covered her frail lifeless body, offering his condolences to the poor unfortunate parents.

To every friend, neighbour and family member, Agnes had finally lost her battle with the long illness which had kept her bedridden for so long. The pain of seeing her crying baby was too much for Edith to bear, it was to her, a huge burden, and a harsh reminder of the unforgivable and sinful affair between that despicable, cheating Kingsley, and her precious vulnerable daughter. In her grief and desperation, and in her strong desire of wanting Kingsley to suffer too, Edith took the small screaming bundle, along with a quickly written note, leaving her in a basket outside the tradesmen's entrance of Kingsley's house.

Nothing would ever be the same for Edith and Stanley. The gloomy dark shadow which eclipsed their life was made worse by the feeling of guilt and regret they had for abandoning their granddaughter. Edith had returned a few days later, in order to retrieve the baby, only to be told by a maid, that the young infant had been taken away. On the many times that Edith continued to call at the house, Kingsley refused to see her, until finally she was told that if she didn't stop making a nuisance of herself, they would call the police. Edith's depression worsened. Stanley was working long hours on the family business to keep himself occupied, while Edith would spend her days sitting deep in thought about Agnes and the baby. It was only after she eventually confided in Martha, telling her everything that she slowly began to climb out of her dark hole. Martha found her a new job and encouraged her to start saving again for the move she had always dreamed of. The two sisters spent more time together, occasionally watching a play in the theatre. It was like old times, except that they could no longer sneak in, but had to pay for their tickets.

Martha arrived at the Eagle Gentlemen's club just as huge flakes of snow began to gently descend. Exchanging a quick greeting with the porter, she got to work quickly. She had too many worries on her mind today. As proud as she was that, like Edith, she had also escaped the overcrowded and rat-infested tenement buildings and was now living in a small terraced house, she would not be happy until all of her family were settled.

Bill and Tom seemed to have disappeared from the face of the earth. What was it with the men folk in her family? Why couldn't they just stay put, she thought. Bill could look after himself, he took after his father. She just hoped that he wasn't breaking the law somewhere, but Tom was weak in body and mind, and a constant worry to her. The sooner they both found good wives to take care of them the better. As she vigorously worked the beeswax into the already glossy wooden surfaces, she prayed for the safe and quick return of her boys, and that they weren't locked up in jail somewhere.

CHAPTER SIXTEEN

Martha hurried home from work, feeling cold and tired. She couldn't wait to put her feet up in front of the fire, with a hot cup of tea. Catching sight of Rose, her neighbour, Martha hoped she wouldn't want to stop and chat this morning.

"Morning Martha, bloody freezing ain't it," Rose shouted as she neared her, "I see yer young men are back 'ome again. Which one's got himself a pretty wife then?"

Martha's expression was one of surprise on hearing this.

"Oh me an' me bleeding mouth," exclaimed Rose, "sorry my darling, I bet yer didn't even know they was back, did yer? Anyway, can't stop an' chat love, our Daisy's gone in ter labour, God 'elp 'er, number seven!" Looking to the sky and rolling her eyes, Rose sped past leaving Martha somewhat relieved that she couldn't stop and chat, especially after the news that she had just reported.

Martha could hear their familiar voices as soon as she walked through her front door, and was forced to wrap her shawl across her nose, trying to block out the terrible smell which had filled her home, and which was obviously coming from her sons. She wondered who in their right mind would want to marry anyone with such a disgusting stench attached to them if there was any truth in what her neighbour had just told her. It wouldn't be the first time that Rose had put two and two together and come up with five, she thought to herself.

"Ma!" exclaimed Bill, as he suddenly appeared in the narrow hallway, his arms set to embrace her.

"Where the bloody Hell have you come from, you smell worse than the Thames, and where's Tom?"

"Well, that's a fine welcome 'ome to yer long lost son ain't it? Come on in Ma, I made yer a nice cup of Rosie Lee. I knew you'd be 'ome soon." Bill was trying hard to be as sweet as he could to his ma. It wasn't easy; he knew he was going to be in the firing line when she saw what a sorry state Tom was in. Brushing away Bill's outstretched arms, Martha walked into the dimly lit back room, where Tom was sprawled out on the brightly coloured rag rug, in front of the glowing fire, he looked pale and thin.

"Ma! I've missed yer so much Ma, an' I've been right poorly, ain't I, Bill?"

"Yeah, 'e 'ad a bit of an accident, but I took good care of 'im, didn't I, Tom? If it weren't fer me, I don't fink 'e would 'ave survived."

Tom didn't answer as Martha just stood staring from one to another, wondering why her sons had turned out to be such thorns in her side.

"Sit down Ma," enticed Bill, as he held out a cup of tea to his ma.

With a heavy sigh, Martha sat down at the table opposite Bill, "Now tell me what you two have been up to since you left home without so much as a goodbye, all those weeks ago. Don't you two thick heads ever think that your ma worries about you when you just up and disappear like that, without a word? I'm warning you now, I don't want one single lie to spill from your mouths, and as soon as you've convinced me, you can both take yourselves to Whitechapel and have a bath. You should know by now, that I'm a cut above all the filth and squalor that surrounds us, and if you want to carry on sleeping under my roof, you had better try and match up to the levels which I expect." Martha placed two pennies down on the table, and folded her arms, waiting for her son's explanation to begin.

"You can't 'alf talk bloody posh, Ma," Bill sniggered, only managing to rile Martha even more.

Bill knew that this was going to be a difficult task, his ma was always able to tell when he was lying to her, so he decided he would just omit a few truths. Telling her that he was offered a handsome reward to deliver some important documents to a toff in a grand house in Cheshire, he then repeated the story which he had told the Milton's, about Tom accidentally setting a barn on fire, and how he then spent time working on the farm until Tom had recovered enough to make the journey back home. Martha's eyes remained firmly fixed on him throughout his whole explanation. She didn't believe half of it.

"Now tell me, which toff with an ounce of sense in his head would pick a rough-looking scoundrel like you to deliver his important documents?" questioned Martha, crossly, "I wasn't born yesterday you know!" Bill scratched his head nervously,

"Well, 'appen it were me tough and fearless looks which got me the job, I look like I can take care of meself, an' no one ain't gonna mess with me."

Still totally unconvinced, Martha turned her attention to Tom,

"So Tom, who bandaged your hands up like that, because I know for a fact that it wasn't our Bill, was it." Pulling himself up, Tom looked at his ma, and then to Bill, whose beady eyes pierced into him. Martha could smell a rat. As Bill looked poised to jump out of his chair, Martha couldn't help but notice his tensed face and clenched fists.

"It was Mrs Milton, on the farm," said Tom quietly, before lying back down and closing his eyes.

"You two had better not be lying to me," warned Martha. "I bumped into Rose from number fourteen, she seemed to think that one of you had got married for some reason....what was all that about then?"

"Oh Ma, you know what that stupid old mare's like, I don't know why yer give 'er the time of day," laughed Bill, trying to make light of what his ma had heard.

Martha gave orders for Bill and Tom to hurry to the communal baths, before she passed out from their unbearable fumes, while she began to tidy up the mess which they had succeeded to make in the short time they'd been home. It was good to see them home safely, she thought, but their long story remained a puzzle to her, which she intended to get to the bottom of. She would have to tackle Tom when he was on his own.

May opened her eyes to darkness, apart from the narrow glint of light which shone from the borders of what looked like a small square door, high above her. Feeling groggy, her head ached, and her limbs felt like lead. Shivering, she felt frozen through to the bone. Her mouth was dry, and there was a disgusting rancid odour which smelt like rotting flesh, causing May's empty stomach to turn over and making her feel sick. Her wrists and ankles were stinging from the tightly bound ropes, and she could feel the taught gag cutting into her flesh.

Having no clue as to where she was, she tried hard to remember what had happened to her, but the last image that came to her mind, was of the tea rooms in Chester, and Bill forcing her to drink the drugged tea. As the cold and damp, stone floor beneath her was causing her muscles to cramp up, May wriggled, trying to relieve the pain. Trying to stay as calm as she could, she knew she could do nothing, but lay and wait, and pray that somehow she might be rescued. Closing her eyes, she tried to imagine it was a gloriously hot summer's day; she was sitting with her dear ma in a beautiful poppy field near her cottage. Ma had baked a delicious sponge cake and made refreshing lemonade. Jack was walking towards her, smiling lovingly as he handed her a small posy of wildflowers. As the tears trickled down May's face and onto her stone pillow, the small square door suddenly opened. As the light poured into May's prison, making her squint from the sudden brightness, Tom walked hesitantly down the stone stairs, after closing the hatch behind him. From the light of his candle, May was now able to see the whole of the damp cellar. She was surrounded by mouse droppings, along with a huge rotting rat, just a few inches from her head. Wriggling in vain, May desperately wanted to be free from her ropes, she wanted to scream and cry. She just wanted to be free of this Hell hole and be back in Ashley Green. As Tom approached her, she felt nervous, wondering what his intentions were.

"I'm sorry me brovver put yer down 'ere....please don't make a noise if I untie you." It was a gentle order, but as May looked into his face, she could tell that Tom was the kind brother, and he did want to help her.

"Where am I?" whispered May, after Tom had removed the tight gag and set to untying the ropes around her wrists and ankles.

"Yer in me 'ome, in London."

"London!" exclaimed May, forgetting that she was supposed to be quiet.

"Shhh, Bill will kill me if 'e finds out what I'm up ter."

"Sorry Tom, and thank you," expressed May. "What's he going to do with me?"

"Better yer don't know, but I'm gonna get yer out of 'ere, you'll 'ave ter wait till it's all clear, an' it's gonna 'ave ter be at night." Tom took out a cold baked potato from his pocket, along with a bottle filled with cold tea. "Sorry it's all cold; I'll try an' get yer something else later."

May thanked him again, before drinking the tea; it was sweet and soothing on her dry throat. Hungrily she ate the potato; it had been a long time since her last meal. Feeling more optimistic about the dire situation she was in, she prayed that Tom would succeed in his mission to free her before she fell into the clutches of Bill with his evil plan.

After Tom had scraped the offending rotting vermin into a metal pale, turning it upside down in the corner of the cellar, he left May with the candle burning, assuring her that he'd return as soon as possible.

May sat for a while, toying with the impulse she had, to make a dash for it up the flight of stone stairs, and trust her chances of making her own quick escape, but decided she would wait a little longer, and hope that Tom knew what he was doing, besides, she thought, the door was most probably bolted from the outside. At least she was no longer in darkness and had had food and drink. She curled herself up into a ball, trying to keep warm.

Bart and jack had arrived at Euston railway station and were in awe of the crowds and the hustle and bustle of London. The accelerated pace of life in the city made them feel quite out of place. Stan had decided that he couldn't leave his young family alone, so remained in Cheshire. The money which the Squire had given them would last longer between two, he had said, and he promised he would keep an eye on poor old Mary Weaver in their absence. Their first port of call was to the offices of Fenwick, Fenwick, and Montague, to enlighten the solicitor on the recent events which had occurred up in Cheshire. Bart had no trouble remembering this name from the letter heading belonging to Emma, now they just had to find out where the offices were situated. They guessed that it would be near the Kingsley's home in Belgravia, so decided to take a hansom cab, hoping that the driver would be familiar with the name.

Time passed painfully slowly for May. Tom had not returned, and curiosity had forced May to climb the steps to the wooden hatch, where her guess was proved correct, the small door was locked from the outside. Pacing backwards and forwards, which was a total of four paces each way, trying to keep warm, May couldn't sit still any longer. Her teeth wouldn't stop chattering, and the sound of vermin scurrying around in the dark corners of the cellar was making her extremely nervous, especially if they were the same size as the one she had seen earlier. Her thoughts turned to those back in Cheshire, which seemed so far away from her now. She hoped that Mrs Weaver was keeping well, and wasn't worrying herself sick about her. Dear Aunty Mary, she thought, she had been so kind. May smiled when she remembered sweet little Jenny, who she missed so much, such a chatterbox, and so clever for her young years. She had realised that Bill was a villain, if only the adults had taken her seriously, then maybe everything would have turned out differently. She was right to call him a monster.

May was bought out of her reverie by the sound of raised voices from up above, along with the clatter of smashing crockery and furniture scraping and banging on the floorboards, there was certainly a loud commotion going on in the house. Climbing up the stone steps, May perched herself near the top, and sat motionless, trying to make out what was being said in the noisy row. Bill's booming voice was full of aggression.

"One bloody word to Ma an' it will be the last word that ever leaves yer mouth; get what I mean?" Bill grabbed Tom from behind, twisting his arm backwards. As he howled in pain like an injured hound, Bill held the sharp blade of a razor close to his throat, while he made his threats. "I swear I'm gonna bloody kill yer one day Tom, yer make me so angry with yer stupid, girly ways. When yer gonna realise that yer can't trick me, cos I know 'ow yer stupid, pathetic little brain works Tom, an' I'm watching every move yer make, got that!"

Pulling Tom's arm backwards even further, in the bid to force a word of agreement from his mouth, Tom suddenly kicked backwards with all the strength that his weakened legs could muster, catching Bill off guard. As Bill lost his footing, Tom quickly grabbed the razor from his hand, turning it around to within an inch of Bill's face. Bill was shocked, he had never witnessed his little brother show any kind of aggression towards him in all his life, it almost made Bill want to laugh out loud, but with the sudden change in Tom's character, and with the sharp blade hovering so close to his face, he decided to keep quiet until he could switch the situation around. Tom had shocked himself that he had managed to overcome Bill for the first time ever. He wanted him to feel what it was like to be at the receiving end of a threat and suddenly became more confident.

"We're gonna let May go free, Bill. It ain't worth all the trouble. She's just a kid, and she ain't done nuffing ter deserve what yer got in store for 'er." Swallowing hard, Tom knew that at any moment, Bill was likely to overpower him.

"Tom, let's sit down an' talk this over before

Ma gets 'ome," pleaded Bill in his kindest voice. Tom hesitated, unsure of how to handle Bill's suggestion.

"We ain't sitting down for any cosy talk, Bill; I might be stupid, but not that stupid."

"Listen, Tom, think about it, if we let little miss sweet 'n' innocent down there go free, yer can bet yer life she'll open 'er sweet mouth, an' before yer can count ter three, we'll be swinging from the end of a rope. Is that what yer want Tom...well is it?" he shouted.

"No Bill, she won't talk, we'll make 'er promise," he replied to Tom convincingly. Blade at his throat or not, Bill could no longer hold in his strong urge to laugh in Tom's face.

"Oh, yer a number one prize idiot, Tom, yer should 'ave stayed up there on the farm; yer as bloody daft as those dumb peasants!"

"I've already untied 'er Bill, an' given 'er some grub too," Tom felt the need to aggravate Bill further and knew this would anger him even more. Bill couldn't take any more. He suddenly took a firm grip on Tom's arms, just above the elbows, shaking him violently until the razor dropped to the floor, all the while, Tom frantically kicked in every direction, but his crazed attack made no impact on Bill. Shoving Tom to the ground, he made a rush to the cellar door.

"I'll show yer, Tom Haines," yelled Bill, as he pulled the bolt across the cellar door, still holding the razor in the other hand...Martha suddenly appeared in the doorway, shocked at what she was seeing.

"What will you show him, Bill?" she demanded angrily, glancing around at the damage they had inflicted in her once orderly home.

CHAPTER SEVENTEEN

George Fenwick had never trusted Quinton Kingsley, his father had been more of a decent sort, even though he tended to bend the rules on many occasions, but at least his heart was in the right place. After sitting with Mr Bart Turrell and his son, and hearing what they had to say, he was left with a sour taste in his mouth, as their story only confirmed that his doubts about that man were not just a figment of his imagination. He just hoped that he wasn't too late for May Huntley and that she remained alive and unharmed. This was now a very serious matter, and George had decided that he must inform the police, though he doubted there was much that they could or would do. To search for one young woman in the overcrowded slums of the East End, would not be top of their priorities. Prostitution, murder, and theft were rife in that area, half the peelers were too squeamish to even venture into this corrupt and seedy underworld of London. There was probably no solid proof that Quinton was involved at this stage, and because of his status in society, he remained unapproachable. George was putting all hope on the Turrell men. At least he had been able to assist them in finding decent lodgings while they remained in London. His clerk's mother ran a small boarding house, which his clerk assured him, was inexpensive and clean. George was fuming; if there was one type of man he couldn't abide; it was a liar and a cheat, and Quinton Kingsley fell into both of those categories. He would definitely not be placing any funds into his account in a hurry.

Mrs Baxter's appearance wasn't at all similar to that of her tall, gangly son. She was short and plump, with a jolly nature, and a warm welcoming smile, who fussed over her lodgers like a Mother hen. Bart and Jack were pleased to have been recommended to such a homely and reasonably priced room in Paradise Street, which although quite basic, was bright and fresh and had everything they needed. Mrs Baxter cooked breakfast and an evening meal for her paying guests, which she served in her clean, and smartly decorated dining room. The six small, square tables were covered with a crisp gleaming white, starched tablecloth, each one having a small vase in the centre, holding a single flower. The silver cutlery shone, along with the six neatly placed silver cruet sets. She ran her boarding house as if it were one of London's huge fancy hotels, but on a much smaller scale.

Since it was now late afternoon, Bart suggested that they wait until the morning before continuing their investigations, and their search for May. It was fast becoming dark, and George Fenwick had warned them of the thick fog which engulfed the City at this time of year, making visibility virtually impossible. Although Jack felt it was wise to agree with his pa, he was frustrated and desperate to venture out in search of May and was feeling utterly useless hanging around with nothing to do. George Fenwick had mentioned to them that if they could locate Kingsley's butler, who had recently resigned, he might be able to provide them with some valuable information. But, thought Jack, that would be like looking for a needle in a haystack, especially here in London where it was so populated.

Martha's arrival home couldn't have been better timed. The shock of seeing her two grown men tearing into each other, waving a sharp blade around dangerously, and at the same time destroying her home, caused Martha to explode in a fit of rage.

"Who or what have you got hidden down in the cellar!" she demanded, screaming at the top of her voice. "What the Hell has got into you two? There's been something fishy going on since you got back home, and I want to know what it is."

Bill knew immediately that his ma was beyond consoling. Placing the blade down, he was alarmed by the state of the house. The table was upturned onto a pile of smashed crockery and a puddle of tea, with one of the chairs missing a leg. Everything was out of place. Tom sat undignified against the scullery doorway, his pale face taught with frustration and anger.

"He's got a girl down there, Ma," announced Tom, quickly, before Bill had the chance to tell her another pack of lies. Bill's cold glare made Tom cower, he knew that he wouldn't be spared his wrath later, but he was relieved that the secret was out.

"Oh Dear God in heaven, help us....what have you gone and done Bill?" Martha knew that Bill got up to some shady dealings, but to be keeping some poor girl, against her will, locked up in the cellar, was just too much for her to comprehend. She marched towards the cellar door, pushing Bill out of her way, angrily. On hearing the sound of the cellar bolt being pulled across the door, May quickly sped back down the steps, blowing out the dwindling candle, and tucking her hands behind her back, giving the appearance that they were still tied up. Martha peered down into the dark cellar, as May sat motionless, barely breathing.

"Don't tell me you've tied her up too?" Martha's question was aimed at Bill, who was still glaring harshly at Tom.

"She ain't tied up no more," Tom muttered, under his breath, as Martha continued to look down into the black hole, feeling guilty about her son's unacceptable behaviour.

"It's alright my dear, everything is going to be

alright now, you're safe my dear, just come on up here," Martha coaxed, hoping that she wouldn't have to take a trip down into the cellar, that she detested, and had only ever been down there once, which was more than enough. Cautiously, May climbed up the stone steps, much to the relief of Martha, who held out her hand to assist her, smiling kindly in the hope to ease her nervousness, and make it clear to her that she didn't approve of Bill's dreadful behaviour. May was aware of how terrible she must look. Her dirty, stained, and crumpled dress had now been on her for days, and she hadn't brushed her hair nor washed. She was physically and mentally drained from the lack of sleep and food and the sheer fear that she had been subjected to. When she was safely out of the cellar, Martha pulled her gently towards her, wrapping her arms around May in a comforting embrace.

"You poor girl," she said in a soft and soothing voice, "I must apologise for my son's despicable behaviour; I thought that I had two adult men, but they have proved to be worse than wild animals." As she led May into the room at the front of the house, away from Bill and Tom, who were sat gawking, the strain of the past few days suddenly hit May, causing her to break down in floods of tears, her slight figure shaking uncontrollably. Martha was feeling so ashamed that her sons had managed to afflict so much distress on to such a sweet young girl, and as she took May under her wing, she reeled out a number of orders to Bill, warning him that if he failed to oblige, he'd find himself homeless. Realising the seriousness in his ma's tone of voice, like a soldier under his officer's command, he got stuck in straight away. The back room was quickly transformed to normality, with the exception of the broken crockery. A large pale of water was being heated up on the stove for May to wash with, and a fresh pot of tea was being made. Tom was exempt from all chores until his health had improved. He sat timidly in the armchair, pretending to be asleep, knowing that Bill would be set on paying him back for what had happened today, but feeling elated that May was now free, and that Ma was taking good care of her. Bill was soon carrying a tray of freshly brewed tea into the parlour, as Ma preferred to call it. Much to his annoyance, he felt like the butler. May couldn't look at him as he placed the tray loudly down on the table in front of them, but she knew he would be fuming that his plan had failed, and hoped he wouldn't take all his anger out on Tom. Martha still had her arm wrapped around May's shoulder, gently stroking her hair now and again, and reassuring her that everything would now be alright, and they would return her home to her family as soon as possible.

"Bill!" she suddenly beckoned, "go around to your Uncle Stanley's, and buy us all a meat pie and some mash." Bill reluctantly obeyed another of his ma's orders, feeling humiliated. If he wasn't so

hard up for cash, and if it wasn't so freezing out, he would walk out of his ma's house, and never return. Taking his time, he strolled to the nearby marketplace where his uncle was standing with his barrow.

Meanwhile, Martha helped May to wash, and change into one of her dresses.

CHAPTER EIGHTEEN

As dawn broke over London, the fallen snow had transformed the dingy East End slums to a pure, clean white, bringing a refreshing brightness to the whole area. The heavy snow had fallen continuously overnight, promising to bring everyday life in the City to a standstill. Jack pulled back the thick chenille curtains, feeling dismayed at the sight of the snow-covered streets, knowing it would make their task twice as difficult. Bart was still sleeping, so Jack, who had experienced a restless night, sat quietly wondering where and how May was. He felt sure that she was still alive, hoping that it wasn't just wishful thinking, and prayed that she wasn't suffering, wherever she was. He knew, that the longer it took to find her, the more her life was in danger. It was a harrowing thought that he tried hard to keep to the depth of his mind. He deeply regretted not telling her how much he loved her, and how he envisaged their future together as husband and wife.

Finding it hard to sit still and quiet, and not wanting to disturb his pa, he dressed and left the room. Downstairs, Mrs Baxter was already up, and from the sound of it, was busy in the kitchen. Tapping timidly on the kitchen door, Jack hoped that she might allow him to have an early morning cup of tea. There was no answer. Maybe she was a bit hard of hearing, thought Jack, as he stood nervously by the door, knocking again, slightly harder.

"Who's there?"

"Oh, er, umm, sorry to disturb you...it's Jack Turrell."

The door flew open, and a flour-covered Mrs Baxter, with her sleeves, rolled up and wearing a matching apron and mob cap, stood boldly in the doorway.

"You'll have to speak up lad, me ears aren't as sharp as they used to be. Now, what can I do for you so early in the morning...I hope your bed was comfy enough for you."

"It was very comfy, thank you, Mrs Baxter; it's just that I woke early, and not wanting to disturb my pa, who's still asleep, I was hoping that I might be able to have a cup of tea if it's no trouble, but I can see that you're very busy...maybe I could lend you a helping hand instead."

"You certainly can son; that would be most welcome," exclaimed Mrs Baxter, as she beckoned Jack into her kitchen, pleased to have some company. "Have you looked out of the window this morning....my, we did have our fair helping of snow last night. I don't think that I'll be venturing out in this today."

Mrs Baxter continued to knead the large lump of dough, disappearing every few seconds in a fresh cloud of flour.

"Can you put the kettle on to boil Mr Turrell, I'm

feeling quite parched too, breathing in all of this flour."

"Please, call me Jack, Mrs Baxter," he insisted.

"Right then Jack, the kettle is out in the scullery, there's no need to refill it, there's plenty of water in it. If you could put it on the stove, and get some cups and saucers from the dresser, that would be most helpful, while I just get these loaves into the oven and clean up my mess." As Mrs Baxter issued her instructions to Jack, pointing to the whereabouts of everything he needed, the kitchen was beginning to resemble the snowy streets outside with the amount of flour which dusted everything. "Oh, I'm such a messy cook; you could easily make another loaf of bread from all the flour that's on the floor," she announced, laughing joyfully.

The kitchen was soon clean and tidy, the loaves were baking, filling the kitchen with their delicious aroma, and Jack and Mrs Baxter were thirstily drinking the tea which Jack had made. As they sat chatting, Jack told her a little of why he and his pa had come to London. Mrs Baxter was clearly alarmed and sympathised with Jack.

"That poor young girl, what must she be going through...doesn't bear thinking about. I hope you find her, Jack. I'll pray for her safety, and for the Good Lord to direct you in the right direction to where those awful men have taken her."

"That's very kind of you, Mrs Baxter, thank you."

"So what's your plan," she quizzed, "do you have

any lead at all to follow up, any clues?"

"Well, we hope to find Mr Gascoigne, he used to be the butler to the man I mentioned. Your son's employer seems to think he could be living nearby."

Mrs Baxter jumped out of her chair and quickly opened the oven door, pulling out the three golden-topped loaves and upturning them onto the table in front of Jack. "Mr Gascoigne you say," her brow wrinkled as she appeared to be in deep thought. "It might be a long shot, but there's a woman I often talk to at the market, who runs a lodging house, and just last week she was singing the praises of her newest lodger, telling me how clean and meticulous he was; she put it down to the fact that he had spent most of his life in service as a butler. Don't think she mentioned his name though. Well, if she did, I don't recall what it was, having said that, I don't even know what her name is. Now, what day was that?" As she sat back down again, looking quite troubled as she battled with her memory, Jack couldn't help thinking how she reminded him of Mrs Weaver.

"That's it," she declared with a look of relief, "it was last Friday because I brought some real tasty fish, so it must have been Friday."

"It's Friday today!" exclaimed Jack, excitedly.

"Maybe she'll be there today. Her lodger must be Mr Gascoigne; it's too much of a coincidence for it not to be him."

"Yes that might be Jack, but as I said, there's no

possible way I'm going out in this treacherous weather, besides, as I said, it's probably something of nothing."

"I'll carry you there," announced Jack.

Mrs Baxter burst into a fit of uncontrollable laughter, making her eyes water as she rolled back her head.

"You're a funny one, Jack. I haven't laughed so much in a long while, that's certainly made my day. Can you imagine what a spectacle that would be, that's if you could actually carry me, which I doubt; all the way to the market!"

"How about me and Pa walking either side of you with the support of our two arms to hold on to, then," suggested Jack, desperate to follow any lead which might bring him closer to finding his dear May.

"Oh, go on with you...Oh, my goodness; look at the time, my guests will be coming down demanding their breakfasts soon. I'm way behind."

"Don't you worry about a thing, Mrs Baxter, I'll help you, just tell me what to do, but please, just give my idea a bit of thought. I'd be forever grateful."

"You know that there's no guarantee she'll be there this Friday, Jack," warned Mrs Baxter.

"I know, but I have to grab every possibility, you do understand, don't you Mrs Baxter?"

"I know, Son," she agreed. "Well, we'll have to see what the weather's doing after breakfast. But I'm not making any promises."

"That's fine, thank you, Mrs Baxter," exclaimed

Jack, feeling more optimistic.

Jack was eager to tell his pa the latest, and so far, only possible lead in the search for May, so after he'd helped as much as he could in assisting with the breakfast preparations, he hurried back up to their room. Bart had woken up and was already dressed. As he'd been wondering where Jack had disappeared to, it was a welcome sight to see him again.

"Ahh, Son, I was worried that you'd gone out in this by yer self, where have yer been then?"

"Come on Pa, let's go down and have breakfast, and I'll tell you about my morning breakthrough. Oh, and, make sure you look your best, you might have to charm an elderly woman into walking out in the snow with us."

Bart looked puzzled at Jack, who had a cheeky grin across his face, but, thought Bart, it must be something positive, since it was the first smile he'd seen on his son's face for a long time.

It didn't take much persuasion; Mrs Baxter had taken to Jack and wanted to do all she could to help find the young girl, who Jack was so obviously in love with. By nine-thirty, all three of them, with Mrs Baxter safely in the middle, were linked in arms, and walking carefully through the thick carpet of snow, towards the aptly named Friday Street. The whiff of fish soon filled their nostrils before even setting sight of the market.

"You should count yourself fortunate that it's not a

hot summer's day, and then you'd have something to wrinkle your noses up to," declared Mrs Baxter, amused at Jack and Bart's contorted faces.

The bad weather hadn't deterred the shoppers from venturing out to the market, every stall saw crowds flocking to purchase their produce.

Costermongers were selling virtually everything, from haberdashery to cakes and sweets, from cuts of crimson and white meat, piled high, to baskets filled with a colourful array of vegetables and fruit. The delicious smell of roasting chestnuts wafted through the air and all around was the sound of the traders screaming out the produce they were selling along with the price. Young girls stood shivering as they held out boxes of matches for sale to passersby, many of them without shoes on their small feet and barely a rag to cover their thin undernourished bodies. Then there were the many fish stalls, which proved to be extremely popular as they sold everything from the Londoners' favoured eels, whelks and cockles to herrings, sprats, and haddock. Mrs Baxter warned them to be on their guard and keep an eye out for pickpockets, as her eyes scanned the market in search of the woman who she was acquainted with. Jack walked around the market purchasing the items which Mrs Baxter needed, while she stood with Bart to one side, eagle-eyed and vigilant.

After a very long hour of standing out in the sub-zero temperatures, they were all feeling disconsolate from their failed attempt to find the woman, who was the one tiny hope they had on a lead to find May.

"Come on," said Bart, "let's call it a day, Mrs Baxter has been a real hero standing out here in the freezing cold trying to help us, it's time we got back before we all get frostbite."

Disappointedly, they left the marketplace, making their way back with Mrs Baxter's, conversation at a minimum. Once again, she walked in the middle, holding both Jack and Bart's arms, while they both carried her shopping, which they'd insisted on paying for, by way of a thank you for her kind help.

"I don't believe it," exclaimed Mrs Baxter, suddenly, as she came to an abrupt halt. "That's my acquaintance, look, she's heading towards us...Oh, thank you, God," she declared, looking up to the Heavens.

Bart and Jack waited anxiously to one side of the road, while Mrs Baxter chatted briefly, before turning to face them, with a beaming smile which lit up her pale blue eyes.

"He's your man, he's Mr Gascoigne, and what's more, he's at home at number seven Windsor Avenue, which is just a stone's throw away."

Mrs Baxter was almost singing her news with elation, she was so excited. Bart and Jack both hugged her spontaneously, making her blush with embarrassment.

"Hey, steady on now you two, I've got my reputation to think of you know. What will folk say," she laughed.

CHAPTER NINETEEN

It had been the first time in a long while that May had felt warm and safe, and had managed to have a good night's sleep. Waking up next to Martha, she was feeling refreshed and optimistic about planning her journey back home. Since she was in London though, she had decided to pay a visit to the solicitor at Fenwick, Fenwick, and Montague before returning to Cheshire. Martha was lying awake, there were too many thoughts swimming around in her head, and she was feeling strangely uncomfortable. Was she going crazy, she thought to herself, because never before had she met anyone who even came close to resembling her dear late niece, Agnes, but this young May was the image of her, not just in appearance, but in her graceful manner too. It was uncanny. With no chance of having a proper talk with May last night, as she was so weary, and found it impossible to keep her eyes open after their meal, Martha thought she'd go and make some tea, light the fire, and settle down for a proper talk with May. If anything, she needed to know how much trouble her boys were likely to be in too....boys, she laughed, they were both in their thirties and should be married with their own families by now, but instead they were running riot through the land, kidnapping, thieving and God knows

169

what else....where had she failed as a Mother, she thought, sadly.

"Good morning my love, did you have a good night's sleep," questioned Martha, as she rose from the bed, wrapping an enormous expensive-looking shawl around her trim figure.

"Good morning Mrs Haines, yes thank you, I'm feeling so much better today," replied May, staring at Martha's elaborate shawl, which reminded her of an intricate tapestry she had once seen in a book at school.

"My friend from the theatre gave me this," announced Martha, reading May's thoughts as her eyes were firmly fixed on the garment. "Oh, and May my dear, please, call me Martha."

"I couldn't do that, it would be too disrespectful."

Smiling, Martha said, "How about Aunty Martha, then, would that suit?"

May, returning the smile, nodded affirmatively.

"Right then, I'm going to make us a nice brew, and try and put some heat into this icebox of a house. Why don't you stay in bed and rest up a bit longer," suggested Martha as she pulled back the heavy ruby-red velvet curtains. "Oh no," she exclaimed, "we've had the world's helping of snow delivered to us during the night, no wonder it's so blooming cold."

May jumped out of bed to take a look, hoping that Martha was exaggerating.

"Oh, this is too much snow, you're right," she uttered, downheartedly, "I won't be able to make it to the end of the street, let alone to Cheshire."

"Don't you worry your pretty little head now, the Londoners will be out there like a swarm of busy bees. They'll soon have all this cleared away so that they can go about their trading and money-making. Now, let me go and put the kettle to boil."

May sat in the large elegantly dressed bed, thinking how hard it was to believe that Martha was the Mother of Tom and Bill. Martha's bedroom was splendidly decorated in rich, warming hues of vermilion. The fine, wooden wardrobe and matching dressing table had obviously been well cared for, with their glossy surfaces, smelling of beeswax. The floorboards were covered with three matching thick, flower-printed rugs which were placed around the bed, and there were beautiful porcelain ornaments placed on a small, red chenille-covered shelf. Sitting proudly on top of the dressing table was a lavish intricate, silver framed mirror, and a slender wash basin and jug, patterned with miniature red rose buds. Martha was definitely a lady with exceptionally good taste, thought May...what a shame that her sons were so uncouth, and such a discredit to her.

A timid cream and ginger cat crept charmingly into the bedroom, jumping up onto the bed with a quiet, brief meow, her eyes firmly fixed on May. As she reached out to stroke her, the cat rubbed her tiny head against May's knuckles, purring contently.

"You must be a cat of leisure," May whispered to

her, as she rubbed the cat's neck, "there's a whole army of mice running loose down in the cellar you know." Blinking slowly at May, she curled up into a ball, neatly tucking her tail in, and closed her eyes. "Oh, there you are, Peaseblossom," declared Martha, as she entered the bedroom carrying a tray of tea and fruit cake. The cat opened one eye reluctantly and glanced lazily at Martha before falling back to sleep.

"That's an unusual name for a cat."

"She followed me home one day from the theatre," explained Martha, "me and Edith, that's my sister, had just watched a performance of A Mid Summer's Night's Dream, so I named her after one of the fairies...don't ask me why, she certainly doesn't do anything magical, in fact, she's a lazy lap cat...doesn't even catch the mice!"

"She's very friendly, and such a pretty colour too," expressed May.

"Well, she's certainly taken to you, May...just as I have. If I spend the rest of my life apologising for the terrible behaviour of my sons towards you, it won't be sufficient. I don't know what in the world possessed them. I hope that they didn't touch you at all May." Martha looked seriously at May, praying that her sons hadn't done anything to ruin this sweet young girl.

"No," replied May, blushing slightly.

"Well, thank God for that," she said, with a sigh of relief, as she passed May a cup of hot, sweet tea.

"I don't make a habit of having tea and cake in bed

May, but I thought it would give us a good chance to talk without any disturbance from those two... they wouldn't dare enter my room, it's strictly out of bounds to them, so you don't have to worry none."

Taking the tea, May felt a sense of sadness for this poor woman, whose sons had failed her. She was going to have to tell her that it was down to them that her beloved ma had died in such an awful way. Whether it could be proved or not, was difficult to tell, but it would surely hurt Martha to find out what her sons were capable of.

"Now," said Martha, making herself comfortable, "tell me about yourself and your family in Chesh...Chesh...Ham, is it?" "Cheshire," May corrected. "I come from a small hamlet called Ashley Green, which is in Cheshire, where until about five weeks or so ago, I was living happily with my dear ma in our lovely little cottage. That was until that awful, awful night when our sweet home was set on fire...deliberately, and my poor ma perished." Martha took a sharp intake of breath, looking compassionately at May.

"Oh, no May, that's terrible...and both Bill and Tom have burns to their hands...how could they, I'm so, so sorry May, your poor mother...poor *you!*" Martha's expression couldn't hide the anguish that she was feeling on hearing this harrowing news.

"A few days later, I found out some shocking news about my ma. I was told by my Aunty Mary...well, she's not a real aunt by blood, but just as good as, and I now live with her. She told me about my real father, who was a man of some wealth, who wanted to leave me something in his will when he died. He died about nine months ago, but it seemed, that someone wanted me and my ma out of the picture...dead in fact. I also found out that my dear late ma was not the woman who bore me, although to me, she will always be my ma, and I know she loved me as I loved her." Pausing to drink the tea, which was fast going cold, Martha had one thought in her head, which seemed such an impossibility, that she daren't dwell on it.

"You poor, poor girl, you have been suffering so much, and then my sons came along, and dragged you all the way down here to London, and in such an ugly manner."

"My real father actually lived in London," announced May, "I have a letter at home from his solicitor, who is also in London, so since I'm here, I intend to pay him a visit before returning home."

"Then you know your father's name, then," questioned Martha, trying to hide her excitement.

"Jeremiah Kingsley," they said in unison, as Martha quickly snatched the cup from May's hand, and wrapped her arms around her, tears streaming down her face.

May hadn't a clue what was going on, and how Martha could possibly know the name of her father.

"From the moment I first saw you, I had my suspicions. I said to myself, that I've never seen

174

anyone with such a likeness to our dear Agnes. You could be her twin, God rest her beautiful soul, it's remarkable, just remarkable." Releasing her firm hold on May to wipe away her tears of joy, May was still left puzzled.

"Just wait till I go and bring Edith to see you, she's going to be elated, she gave up all hope of ever seeing her granddaughter again, years ago...Oh, this is indeed a day to remember."

As Martha hugged May again, Peaseblossom meowed loudly as she jumped down from the bed, and dived underneath it for some peace and quiet.

"I still don't understand, Aunty Martha, what exactly are you saying?" quizzed May.

"Well technically, it's actually, *Great Aunty Martha*, and as sad as I am to say it, those two scallywag sons of mine, are your cousins once removed, but on a brighter note, my dear younger sister, Edith, who you will meet soon, is no other than your grandmother."

Martha couldn't contain her excitement, and couldn't wait to tell Edith the miraculous news. She decided that it would probably be better to tell Edith first on her own, to give her a chance to come to terms with this amazing discovery, before the rest of the family were told.

Downstairs, Tom was huddled in a chair by the fire, still looking grey-faced, and feeling under the weather.

"Where's your brother?" asked Martha, as she

marched passed him on her way to the scullery.

"Don't know Ma…'e went out ages ago."

"Typical," exclaimed Martha, tutting loudly,

"he's never around when you need him."

"What's so important Ma?"

"I wanted him to go and fetch your Aunty Edith around here; I've got some extremely important news to tell her…Could you go instead, Tom?"

"Ma, 'ave yer seen the snow out there, and me boots is full of 'oles too… can't it wait till Bill gets back."

"Well, at least you have a pair of boots, which is more than half the folk have got around here."

Martha had had more than enough of her son's behaviour of late; even Tom was beginning to vex her with his whining ways. She decided to go back upstairs and chat with May…get to know her newly discovered relative properly, before the news was out. She would savour every golden moment of this private meeting, while she still had May all to herself.

CHAPTER TWENTY

At mid-day, May and Martha were still deep in conversation, while Peaseblossom, who had now sneaked into the middle of the bed, was lapping up the attention she was receiving from May's continuous stroking. Martha had been filling May in on every member of her newly discovered family, including the whole affair and tragic death of May's natural mother. May's tears trickled down her soft cheeks as she tried to imagine how devastating that period must have been for her mother and her grandparents. If there was any consolation in the whole terrible business, it was the fact that she had never, or would never meet her father. She wondered how Bill would feel when he found out that she was part of his family....did he have the capability of feeling guilt and regret? ... She doubted it very much, after all, if her half-brother was behind all the sinister goings on, why should it make any difference to Bill that they were related? Tom would be pleased, she thought; deep down May knew that he was a kind, caring and gentle character, it was only his weakness, and the need to follow his older brother which was his downfall. For Martha's sake at least, May hoped that Bill would mend his ways if it wasn't too late. May couldn't wait to meet the rest of her family... how bizarre to suddenly discover a handful of close relatives, so soon after losing her dear ma, who, in fact, turned out not to be related at all, though, to May, she would always be her beloved and much-loved ma. She had sacrificed her whole life to be a Mother to her, and what a remarkable, caring and affectionate Mother she had been.

May told Martha all about her life in the quiet and peaceful hamlet of Ashley Green, about the people in her life, and her love for Jack. She explained to her how she came to be working on the Milton's farm, where she had first seen Bill. Martha was horrified on hearing about her son's inexcusable behaviour and became as worried as May when she voiced her nagging concerns about the safety of Jack's poor father, who Bill had harmed in order to steal his horse and cart, and abduct May. The more they talked, the more convinced she was that before long, Bill would be swinging from the gallows, leaving her with a nasty feeling in the pit of her stomach. Their conversation came abruptly to an end when Peaseblossom leapt from the bed, knocking over a cup and saucer with the swishing of her tail, sending it tumbling to the floor and spilling the remains of the cold tea everywhere.

"*Peaseblossom!*" shouted Martha, theatrically. "You're supposed to move gracefully, like a dainty fairy…what's got into you today?"

May quickly tried her best to clean up the mess, after opening the door, allowing Peaseblossom to make a swift escape.

"I think that's our cue to wash and dress and introduce you to the rest of your family....your grandmother is going to be absolutely ecstatic, and in utter shock when she finds out...I'd better take a bottle of smelling salts with me, just in case... May, help yourself to any garment which fits you from out of my wardrobe," announced Martha, as she took yet another glimpse out of the window.

"Thank you, Aunty Martha; you've been very kind to me."

"Do you think that your young man, Jack is out looking for you May, and do you think that he would come all this way to London? We must try and contact him somehow, to assure him that you're in safe hands."

"I really don't know. He knows that Bill and Tom come from London and that my half-brother and my late father lived in London, but....I just pray that Mr Turrell is alive...oh God, that would be terrible if..."

Martha rushed over to comfort her again, with a reassuring hug. Her own heart was also in turmoil, with the constant nagging worry of how many horrendous, unforgivable crimes her son had committed, and what would be his fate in all of it.

"Why don't I go and bring Edith....I mean your grandmother here...it will save you having to go out in this, and I can tell you're still feeling a tad weak," suggested Martha.

"What about Bill, he might come home, and with

179

you not here, he might do something awful to me, or even kill me...and Tom is so poorly still, he wouldn't be able to protect me." May's sudden erratic outburst made Martha realise how anxious May was still feeling.

"You're right to be worried, my love, I'd be the same if I were in your shoes...no, let's get ready, and I'll take you to meet your dear grandmother, it's only a couple of streets away, and we can leave Tom to rest....he's still not himself."

Nothing could have prepared Lizzie for the shock that she received, on opening the front door to the caller at Quinton Kingsley's residence. As she timidly pulled open the heavy front door, expecting it to be one of her employer's acquaintances, or perhaps Mr Fenwick, who had become a frequent caller of late, Bill rammed the door in her face, sending her flying across the hallway, knocking over the hat and umbrella stand and sending it crashing deafeningly to the floor. Seeing Bill's repugnant, threatening face, Lizzie backed towards the stairs, leading down to the kitchen, terrified for her life.

"Where's the governor," demanded Bill, spitting out his words, his voice roaring. "Where the Hell is bloody Quinton!"

As Lizzie stood up, running screaming down to the safety of Mrs Booth in the kitchen, Quinton broke out into a cowardly sweat on hearing the raging voice of Bill Haines...not a man who Quinton wished to be on the wrong side of. Nervously, Quinton tried to think of a way to console this enraged and dangerous man, who was nearing him. It was too late, Bill stood in the doorway of Quinton's study, his large hideously attired body shaking with pure anger. His scarred face was a bright magenta, partly from the freezing temperature outside, but mostly from the raw aggression which was boiling up in his veins. There wasn't a second for Quinton to think, or speak, as Bill marched right up to him, and grabbed him roughly by his neck, his oversized calloused hand scratching against Quinton's sweating skin. Quinton felt his eyes bulging out of their sockets as he struggled to breathe. Even as his feet lashed out, kicking into Bill's shins, it did nothing but make the hold on his neck tighter, as Bill smirked at him, bringing his face closer, until he was within a whisker of Quinton's face, breathing his rancid breath through decayed and blackened teeth.

"I've done the job, an' now I want me reward...yer bloody pompous bastard," yelled Bill, spitting out his words, as he released Quinton's neck, pushing him violently to the ground.

Coughing and spluttering, Quinton managed to struggle to his feet. His throat felt raw and bruised, causing his voice to be hoarse as he spoke.

"Bill, what's got into you? I've been waiting for you to call on me to collect your reward...do I take it that the deed is done at long last, only I was up in Cheshire myself, and was told, that although Mrs

Huntley sadly perished in a disastrous house fire, her daughter was saved."

As Bill grabbed hold of the heavy iron poker, waving it high above his head, Quinton trembled with fear from his threat.

"If yer don't 'and me over me 'undred pounds, yer a dead man, Quinton. This 'ere poker is just itching ter strike yer stinking fat head, so bloody well pay up…a deal's a deal."

Quinton fumbled around, pulling out all the drawers on his desk, keeping one eye on the poker as it loomed closely above him. All he wanted was for this filthy villain to leave him alone and leave his home.

"Look Bill, can you just place that damn poker down while I find your money…I can't even think under this pressure…don't worry, you'll get your reward, and then I'd appreciate it if you would leave. Your presence is scaring my staff."

"Scaring you more like, yer useless coward. Now, 'urry up, I don't feel right in this bloody posh 'ouse." Bill refused to let go of the lethal poker, as he stood impatiently, hovering over a nervous and shaking Quinton, as he awkwardly retrieved the envelope, containing the said amount.

"Here you are, now take it and get out of my home. I must have been mad to have ever had anything to do with the likes of you." As Quinton handed the envelope over, Bill couldn't stop himself from swinging the poker, striking Quinton heavily on the side of his head, and sending him crashing to the floor, where he lay motionless.

"The likes of me eh! I'll show yer, Quinton bloody Kingsley; what the likes of me can do," he boasted, as he angrily wrenched out every drawer in Quinton's desk, thrusting any money that he came upon deep into his pockets, along with as much silver that he could manage to conceal. Leaving hastily through the front door, which was still open, Bill walked briskly along the street, looking suspiciously out of place in this wealthy area of London.

Turning the corner, as they made their way towards Quinton's house, Jack and Bart couldn't believe their eyes when they saw Bill hastening along the street. They were on their way to confront Quinton, before trying to locate Bill and Tom in the East End, as advised by Mr Gascoigne, who they had spent the past hour with. He had been extremely helpful, especially after hearing how they had been neighbours of Emma Huntley since she'd left London and Jeremiah Kinsley's employ all those years ago. He was stunned and greatly saddened upon hearing of her death, and the suspicious circumstances surrounding it. When Bill's name was mentioned, he immediately remembered the address which he had taken from Quinton's desk but warned them on how dangerous the slums of the East End could be, especially for strangers to the area, and to their ways. Gascoigne knew that these placid country folk were not accustomed to the underworld dens of the villains living in the slums.

As they walked up the few steps to the opened door of Quinton's house, they sensed that all was not well. Lizzie was sitting on a small high backed chair in the wide hallway, crying hysterically, and all that could be heard coming from the study was the wailing voice of Mrs Booth,

"Oh my God, he's killed the master...Oh, Dear Lord, he's dead."

Rushing in through the door and into the study, both Bart and Jack couldn't help feeling that this selfish, heartless man, who was lying so pitifully and undignified on the floor in his luxurious domain, had finally received a measure of what he deserved. Bart could feel a faint pulse, as he placed his fingers on Quinton's neck.

"He's still alive, but only just I reckon," he proclaimed. "Mrs, can you fetch a doctor to him... we are strangers to London, and ..."

Without giving Bart the chance to finish, Mrs Booth was praising the Lord that Quinton was still breathing, and hurrying out of the house to call a doctor.

"I'll fetch the police too," she declared. "He needs locking up and the sooner the better. No one is safe while that monster is at large."

Bart thought it better not to try and move him yet but asked the still-trembling Lizzie to fetch a warm blanket to cover him.

"She's not the first person to call Bill a monster," said Jack, recalling what May had told him about little Jenny Milton.

CHAPTER TWENTY-ONE

Just as Martha had anticipated, the bottle of smelling salts was well and truly needed, as Edith had swooned for the second time in less than ten minutes, from the shock of seeing her granddaughter, who she'd thought, was lost to her forever.

May and Edith sat side by side on the petite brown button-backed sofa in Edith's spotless and orderly parlour. Both May's and Edith's dresses had become saturated from the ankle-deep snow outside, and they'd left a trail of icy droplets throughout the house. Edith was lost for words, but her tears flowed easily, followed by smiles and then more tears, as she held on tightly to May's hand, almost as if she might suddenly disappear if she let go of it. Martha stood by the roaring fire, warming herself, and drying out the hemline of her skirt, as she retold the story of how May came to be sitting alongside her grandmother. As Edith listened intently to her sister, she shared the same shame and shock as Martha had felt, on hearing the full extent of Bill and Tom's involvement in the whole ordeal. She had never envied her sister for having two sons and had always thought of them as being lazy and troublesome, sympathising with her sister as she'd watched her struggle over the years, trying her best to bring them up as good law-abiding citizens, which wasn't an easy task when you lived in the East End slums of London.

Stanley was still out working, and with Christmas only a few days away, the marketplace was extra busy. His popular pies, which were reputed to be the tastiest ones in the East End, were in great demand, especially at this time of the year. With all the dramatic events of late, Christmas had completely slipped Martha's mind, and May had lost track of what month or even what day it was, with all that she had endured over the past weeks.

"I can't believe it, Martha...are you sure I'm not dreaming, it's a miracle, a real bona fide miracle...What's my Stanley going to say, I wonder...you best hold on to those smelling salts, he's sure to pass out," she chuckled, still looking totally dazed.

"Well, I'm going to make us all a cup of sweet tea while you two get to know each other. I don't suppose Stanley left some pies behind, I'm blooming starving, and I dare say May could eat another pie too."

"Another pie?" queried Edith.

"Yes, I sent our Bill out to buy some for our supper last night...that reminds me, you haven't set eyes on him today have you, Edith, only he left home early this morning."

"I haven't seen Bill nor Tom for weeks, Martha, and it's strange that Stanley didn't mention that he served Bill last night because I was only saying, a couple of days back, that I hadn't seen your lads for ages...oh, and yes, there are three full racks of pies on the kitchen table...just warm a couple through."

Not wanting to dwell on the whereabouts of Bill and why Stanley had failed to tell her that he'd seen him, Edith returned all of her attention to May.

Martha felt very unsettled as she busied about in Edith's kitchen. Yet again there was that gnawing feeling deep in the pit of her stomach....she felt panicky, as her heartbeat was thumping out of control, making her feel quite light-headed. Telling herself to stop being so silly, and pull herself together and that it was probably down to the fact she was hungry and tired and had suffered so many shocks recently, she set to preparing the food and making the tea...but she couldn't block out the worrying feeling she had about Bill.

It was late afternoon as Bill emerged from the Dog and Duck inn, having just spent the previous hour or so dwelling on his next move. He knew now that the police would be on his trail. Convinced that he had murdered Kingsley, he knew that it wouldn't be long before they also caught up with May. She would open her mouth, and that would bring about his death sentence...no, he thought, the only solution was to destroy any leads and leave London, maybe even leave the country; after all, he had a small fortune now, thanks to that bloody stuck-up toff...yes, he thought, grinning smugly,

Kingsley deserved to die.

Taking the back streets and alleyways, to avoid being spotted, Bill called into the first ironmonger's shop that he passed, purchasing a bottle of paraffin oil. The small timid looking girl who was selling boxes of matches outside the marketplace shied away on catching a glimpse of Bill's grotesque figure marching towards her.

"Little girl, I ain't gonna do yer no 'arm...give us a box or two of yer matches, an' I'll make it worth yer while," Bill coaxed. The young girl took a step forward, leaving the safety of the dark shadows, as she held out the matches at arm's length, willing Bill to take them, so she could disappear quickly back into the darkness.

"Ta little girl, 'ere yer go, take this ter yer family," declared Bill proudly, as he placed two shining, silver shillings into the palm of her tiny cold hand. Not believing her luck, her small face lit up with a broad, partially toothed smile, as she skipped off in the direction of her home, elated that she would be able to make her family so happy.

"Ta Mister," she shouted over her shoulder.

Continuing through the back streets, Bill was hoping that his ma was out. She normally descended on the market at the end of the day to buy up all the bargains. She prided herself on being a thrifty shopper, with the added skill of haggling prices down to next to nothing when the costermongers were eager to pack up and return home for the night. Bill felt sure that she would have left May at home, as for his brother, if he was there with her, then serve him right, he'd caused nothing but trouble for Bill since the day he was born...he was a weak waster, thought Bill, trying to justify his intended actions. Tom was going nowhere in life, and would only continue to hold Ma back from any future plans that she might have. Coming to a narrow secluded alleyway, Bill felt the need to go over his plans once again. His head was spinning as he reconsidered all the ifs and buts, and the possibilities of what might or what might not be...there was a chance that Kingsley was still alive, and that the fire in Cheshire would be seen as an accident...could he really risk setting fire to his ma's house....what if May kept quiet...even if she talked, and Kingsley was dead, wouldn't he be better off just getting as far away as possible, and hope that he reached a safe destination before the police caught up with him...why risk going back home? The police might already be there if Kingsley was still alive and had told them his address, which he was sure to do. Rubbing the back of his head as he slumped down onto the icy floor, leaning against the brick alleyway, Bill knew that he had to arrive at a decision quickly before it was too late, and he ended up jailed, or even worse.

Following Doctor Taylor's instructions, between them, Bart and Jack had managed, with a struggle to carry Quinton up to his bed, where he lay pale-faced and swathed in bandages around his throbbing head.

Mrs Booth was fussing over him in her usual manner, trying to arrange his extravagant pile of pillows, while at the same time, muttering under her breath, on how he needed to employ more staff for such a large house, and a new butler too. Lizzie was ordered to make sure that a good fire was burning in Quinton's bedroom. Downstairs, Bart and Jack were enlightening the police constable to the full story, which seemed too much for him to take in. He had presumed that this was just a common assault and robbery, but as he stood in Quinton's study making notes, while Jack and Bart frantically tried to recall all of the past events, without omitting any minute detail, he suggested that it would be better if they accompanied him down to the police station, where he was sure that his sergeant would want to hear their statements, and that he would almost certainly arrange for a search party to track down this very dangerous man, and look for the missing girl at the same time before any more crimes were committed. Jack, however, was worried sick that May was still in grave danger, and was intent on making his way to Bill's home address, no matter what dangers lurked in the menacing and overcrowded East End slums. Against Bart's wishes, and his persistent pleas to Jack for them to stick together, he was unsuccessful in persuading him. Jack remained adamant and knew it would be better for his father to remain in safe hands at the police station, rather than to accompany him. Taking a few vague directions from the policeman, who also admonished Jack on the risks of going in search alone, Jack said his farewells to Bart, telling him that he would hopefully meet him back at their lodgings later, in time for their supper.

Sergeant Rawlins, of the Metropolitan Police, was intrigued when he heard of the recent events which had taken place in Quinton Kingsley's home. It was not the first time that his name had been mentioned in the station in the last week, and he felt sure that he would soon have enough evidence to make a couple of arrests, and tie this case up. Mr Fenwick and Mr Gascoigne had both made accusations relating to both Mr Quinton and Bill, respectively. Now, on hearing what Bart Turrell had just revealed, the whole picture was coming into place nicely. In light of the new revelation though, that a decent young girl was involved and had been abducted, and was now in considerable danger, Sergeant Rawlins immediately issued orders for five of his most experienced constables to go in pursuit of Bill, and another constable to keep watch on Mr Quinton Kingsley until he had recovered enough to be bought into the station for a thorough interrogation, just in case he had any ideas of leaving the area.

CHAPTER TWENTY-TWO

Choking on the thick black smoke, Tom crawled up the narrow wooden staircase, in a bid to rescue his ma and May. Bright amber flames surrounded him, bringing back memories of when Bill had started the fire in Ashley Green, and now he had an idea of what it must have felt like for May and her mother. The bannister was scorching hot, and he knew it would be impossible to return down the stairs with his ma and May...they would all have to jump out of the window, and hope to land in a snow drift to cushion their fall...a broken leg would be far better than burning alive, he thought. The angry, raging hot flames were following close behind him as he opened the door to his ma's bedroom, all the while shouting to her, that the house was on fire, and that they all had to evacuate the house quickly; though his croaky voice was barely audible above the noisy crackling, as each flame seemed to be laughing wickedly at him. The whole room was soon engulfed with blinding smoke, which stung like pepper on Tom's eyes, making him squint as he frantically searched for signs of life. The searing heat was becoming too much for him to tolerate and there was no sign of his ma or May. Tom could scarcely breathe as he choked violently on every smoke-filled intake of breath. In a desperate frenzy, he fought with the jammed window, as the flames had now leapt onto his clothing like a merciless killer. Through the ferocious heat and his overwhelming agony, he picked up the heavy framed mirror, and with his last drop of energy, smashed it through the window, plunging head first out behind it, into the inviting cold air.

As the fire brigade battled to contain the fire, throwing bucket after bucket of water onto the blaze, the street was full of neighbours, assisting vigorously, knowing that their own homes were now in peril, should the raging fire spread.

Amongst the crowds which had gathered, stood Jack, in utter shock at what he was witnessing. Feeling useless and devastated as yet another nightmare unravelled in front of him, he rushed to where a crowd had gathered around a still, lifeless body, laying on the frozen ground. As the name, Tom, echoed from every mouth in the crowd, Jack had no doubts that this must be Bill's unfortunate brother, and that yet again, this was the consequence of Bill's evil handy work. The burly-built fireman blocked the doorway with his broad shoulders, as a gathering of women demanded that they searched for Martha, who, they stressed, was bound to be still inside.

"There's nobody else in the 'ouse, now stay back ladies," he demanded. They refused to believe him, continuing to shout and scream hysterically. As Jack took a few steps back, he noticed a cloth being pulled over Tom's face, as a middle-aged man shook his head in dismay, the look of disbelief written on the stunned faces of the neighbours as they collected in small groups along the street. A group of policemen suddenly appeared, running towards the crowd, blowing their whistles noisily, as they pushed their way amongst the crowds.

"Ain't yer got no respect for the dead....there's a young man who's lost 'is life over there," screamed one woman, as she pointed to where Tom lay. "Bloody useless peelers," she continued. There was so much commotion and confusion going on in this impoverished street, as the crowds continued to multiply, that Jack could do nothing but stand in sheer bewilderment. He felt insignificant in this crowd of Londoners; a stranger prying on this private assembly of longstanding friends and neighbours; all he wanted was to find his darling May, and leave these foreign parts, returning to the beautiful green and open fields of Cheshire which he longingly remembered. The vast countryside, where the air was unsullied and where he could walk confidently amongst the familiar places and faces.

Oblivious to what was going on two streets away, the gathering in Edith's house was jolly and relaxed. May had become well acquainted with her grandmother, and they were getting along extremely well, having so much to talk about. May felt as if she had known her grandmother for years, as they talked, deep in conversation; Edith was still astonished as to how May and Agnes were so similar. It was the best day that Edith had experienced in many years. Martha kept the teapot full, and they had all enjoyed feasting on the family's meat pies.

"I don't know why Stanley's so late, business must be brisk," announced Edith as she got up to place some more coals onto the fire. "I'm so excited to tell him, and for him to meet May, that I think I will burst, and if he doesn't show his face soon, I'm going to have to go myself and bring him home."

A heavy-handed hammering on the front door put a sudden end to their casual banter, making all three of them stop and look in alarm at each other, wondering what could be wrong. A young boy wearing an oversized flat cap and ripped trousers, not quite reaching his calves, was anxiously stood outside, hopping from one bare foot to another; he was on the verge of applying his fists once more, when Edith pulled the door open, straight away recognising him to be one of her neighbours' lads, though she couldn't remember his name.

"*Mrs!*" he shouted breathlessly, "me ma says yer ter come quick, yer sister's 'ouse is on fire, quick Mrs, yer should 'urry round there now."

Martha jumped up from her seat on hearing this shocking news, hoping that it was just this lad's idea of a cruel prank or a dare. Within five minutes, Martha, Edith, and May had arrived at a very overcrowded Cromwell Road, where the heavy reek of smoke still lingered in the air, even though the fire had now been extinguished. Neighbours and friends descended on Martha from every direction, some seaming eager to be the bearers of bad news, and others wishing only to give comfort, as they led her to where Tom's lifeless body lay. As she pulled back the grubby scrap of material which covered his face, the pain was unbearable, as she buckled to the ground, letting out strident, shrill cries of despair. She gently cradled her beloved son's head in her arms, willing him to breathe again and open his eyes, as she rocked him to and fro.

Leaning against a wall, Jack still stood observing the crowds and daydreaming about the day when he would return home with his pa, and, hopefully, with his sweet May, which now seemed like a million miles away. Overhearing a conversation between three of the firemen and a constable, one of them holding up an empty paraffin bottle, as they discussed how the fire was almost certainly no accident, Jack instantly knew that this was yet another one of Bill's ruthless undertakings, and now he had murdered his own brother. What were the chances of poor May being alive, he thought to himself dismally?

As the crowds gradually began to disperse, Jack decided to leave and rejoin his pa, who, he thought, should now be back in their lodgings in Paradise Street, though since darkness had fallen, he was unsure of his way back. His eyes rested on a distraught woman, who he thought, must be Bill and Tom's unfortunate mother. She was lovingly comforted by two women. They were assisting her to stand and gently coaxing her away from the lifeless body, which was now covered with his mother's coat. Jack was unable to take his eyes off of one of these women, from the back she reminded him so much of his dearest May; she was the same height, with the same petite shape, and even moved in the same elegant and refined manner as May. As she turned around to face in the direction of Jack, he was taken aback...nothing made any sense to him...was the darkness playing tricks with his eyesight? Had the whole trauma of the day caused his mind to falter? No matter how foolish he might look, and however much embarrassment this would cause to both parties, Jack knew he had to pursue her, and so trailed behind all three women as they slowly began to walk away from the tragic scene, leaving the area.

"May!" he called. But there was no response... *"May, May,"* he frantically shouted, now past caring if he made a complete fool of himself. She turned around, curious shock written on her beautiful face. In that split second, for Jack and May, the entire universe seemed to stand in motionless silence, until she suddenly broke away from her two companions, racing forward towards Jack, his arms outstretched ready to embrace his dear, sweet love, as they held each other closely, tears flowing from both of their eyes in a reunion which Jack had thought would never take place.

"Oh Jack, Jack, I'm so sorry Jack, I'm so sorry....your poor dear father...and it's my entire fault." May's heart-rendering sobs echoed through the street as she struggled to compose herself. It had been an overwhelmingly emotional day for her, and as Jack's strong arms held her, preventing her from collapsing onto the ground, the trauma of everything she had endured became like a burden that she could no longer bear. Martha and Edith, who were now closely huddled together, hobbled toward Jack, as he held May in his arms. He was curious to know who these women were. He had watched them earlier, before he'd recognised May, thinking what a close and loving family they were. "May, my darling, May," Edith soothingly spoke, as she stroked May's pallid cheek. "Thank you so much, young man, she's had a nasty shock... well, we all have." As Edith lovingly gazed at May, Martha's tears trickled down her anguished face, as she gently shook May's arm, and spoke her name. Jack was beginning to feel like an intruder among them, and they obviously had no idea who he was.

"Would you be so kind as to carry my granddaughter to her home...it's in Potts Lane." Shocked by this woman's words, and not having the slightest clue where Potts Lane was, Jack was unable to do anything but just stand still in bewilderment, and confusion. All he wanted to do was to carry May back to the warmth of Mrs Baxter's lodging house and be reunited with his pa...What was this woman saying? He just didn't understand. May's long eyelashes fluttered softly as she opened her eyes and glanced up at Jack, relieved that she hadn't just dreamt that he was here with her at long last.

"May, Thank God...how are you feeling," Jack asked attentively, thankful that she had come to.

"*Jack!*" exclaimed Martha and Edith in unison, "How glad we are to meet you, Jack. May's told us so much about you, and who'd have thought you'd turn up here in London," announced Edith, leaving Jack even more confused, as he gently released May from his arms, allowing her to stand on her feet again.

"I'm afraid it's been a harrowing day, we've sadly just lost my dear nephew, and Martha's beloved son, Tom, and in tremendously distressing circumstances, to say the least."

"I think that we all need to go back to Edith's, and explain to poor Jack here, who we are, and what's been going on," sniffed Martha, tears still filling her eyes.

As she was speaking, two policemen strolled up behind them, notepads in hand, ready to make notes, as they requested to have a word with Martha. At the same time, Stanley appeared, running towards them, worry etched on his tired and troubled face.

"What did you mean, May...about Pa?" asked Jack, while the rest of the party were engaged in answering the constable's questions.

"Pa is fine; he's here in London with me."

"Oh thank God!" cried May. "That's wonderful news...I've had such an awful feeling, that Bill had killed him before stealing me away to this awful place. I can't understand why people are always so infatuated with London; give me Ashley Green any day."

"Oh May, I just want to take you home and spend the rest of my life looking after you. I've been that worried I'd never see you again...Oh May, sweet May, I can't imagine..."

"Then don't, Jack, don't even try to imagine...we've been united again, and I have so much more news to tell you. It could have turned out much worse you know."

Jack had to bite his tongue in order to curb his strong impulse in asking May to marry him. He knew that it was neither the time nor the place, and he intended his proposal of marriage to be a day they would cherish in their hearts forevermore, and remember fondly when they looked back, not this day in the depressingly shady East End slums, with a dead body lying on the ground nearby, and a murderer still at large.

CHAPTER TWENTY-THREE

The tragic death of Tom and the disappearance of Bill overshadowed what should have been a day to celebrate. Edith's parlour had become filled to capacity, not just with neighbours, friends and police constables, but with every raw emotion. The reality of Tom's death seemed to have only just hit Martha, as she sat quietly sobbing in the kitchen, in solitude, even though she knew that she would soon have to answer the long list of questions from the police. Even in the midst of her mourning, she felt vexed with Bill; he had caused her nothing but torment and trouble throughout his entire life, and this was the final straw. She could not tolerate any more of his evil actions. The fact that Tom had left this world not knowing that he was related to May caused her even more grief. She knew how fond he had been of her. Tom's heart was worth ten of Bill's, she thought, and though it pained her terribly, as a Mother, to think in such a way, she wished with all her heart that it had been Bill's body laying dead in the icy cold street.

Stanley was elated when Edith introduced him to May, filling him in quickly with how she had been discovered, but under the present circumstances, and with such a crowd in their home, Edith omitted all the not-so-pleasant details. She would tell him the whole story later when peace and quiet had been restored to her home. Stanley, however, had not needed the smelling salts and declared that he had prayed every day for this miracle to come about and that he had placed all his trust in the Almighty. He was in total amazement at how similar May's appearance was to that of his beloved Agnes and kept finding himself watching her in disbelief, feeling as though the clock had been turned back some seventeen years. The memories of Agnes, and her appalling death, together with the recent loss of Tom, had left Stanley feeling extremely low in spirit. He felt saddened that the arrival of May had coincided with such a calamity, and while part of him felt like taking her by the hands and dancing around the room with her, the shocking death of Tom, served like a heavy iron clamp, holding him down, and suppressing his joy.

Jack was totally astonished when May revealed to him that she was so closely related to Bill and Tom. It was now seriously looking like Bill would be sent to the gallows, providing he was caught, which he prayed would be the case; the thought of him still on the loose, made Jack shudder, he had proved to be brutal and inhumane. How could his sweet, soft-natured May possibly be related to an ogre like Bill, he thought, but tried to brush that thought away, at least her grandparents seemed pleasant enough, and Tom and Bill's mother, who he strongly sympathised with, was not the rough sort of woman with no morals that he'd imagined

Bill's mother to be, but an exceptionally caring, loving, and motherly sort. He was so thrilled for May too, now having a handful of real relatives, after the sad loss of her ma. With all the evidence now pointing at Bill, he was now a wanted man; wanted for murder.

Many of the houses in Potts Lane had kept their curtains drawn out of respect, as a steady trail of friends and neighbours came to say their final goodbyes to Tom, whose body was now laid out in Edith's parlour. Martha had temporarily moved into her sister's house until her home was made habitable again. Jack and May decided it was time to rejoin Bart at Mrs Baxter's lodging house, assuring everyone that they would return the following day.

It was a relief to be away from the bleak and sombre atmosphere of Stanley and Edith's house, and as Jack took May's hand in his, glancing at her lovingly, he felt an inner jubilance and contentment, which he had not felt for a long time, and knew that his pa would be euphoric when they arrived together. The air was bitingly cold and sharp. The full moon shone down on them like a guiding beacon, adorned by an array of bright glittering stars. The snow, now frozen solid like sheets of ice beneath their feet made walking exceedingly hazardous, and slow. They carefully followed the road, concentrating on every slippery step. The only directions which Jack knew, took them into Cromwell Road and past the remains of Martha's house, where to May's delight, Peaseblossom emerged from inside the doorway, gingerly tiptoeing across the snow as she meowed loudly.

"Look, Jack, there's Peaseblossom...Aunty Martha's cat."

"Peaseblossom," laughed Jack, "What sort of name is that for a timid little cat?"

As May gently stroked her, Peaseblossom was clearly pleased to see a familiar friend as she purred noisily, lapping up every second.

"We'll have to take her with us," announced May, assertively, "she must be wondering what's happened to her home and family. She's probably very scared and lonely, and trust me, Jack, I know how that feels."

"Well, I don't suppose Mrs Baxter will object just for one night," assured Jack, thinking that May was overreacting to the plight of a cat being left alone for a night, but put it down to all the traumas she had suffered of late. "But you'll have to hide her underneath your shawl if we manage to find a hansom cab when we reach the main road, I don't think cats are permitted inside of them."

It was late evening when Jack, May, and Peaseblossom arrived on Paradise Street. Bart had been worried out of his mind, thinking the worst, so Mrs Baxter had tried her utmost to console him, finding every plausible reason why Jack had been delayed, and chatting about everything and anything that popped into her head, hoping it would distract Bart's gloomy thoughts, and make the time pass quickly.

As Jack knocked on the door May hid out of sight, clutching Peaseblossom tightly, hoping that she wouldn't suddenly leap out of her arms.

"Jack, my boy," exclaimed Bart, as he pulled his son close, hugging him. "Thank God you're safe, I've been worried out of my mind about you...come on in, out of this bitter night, lad. I've 'ad every worst scenario possible going through my head; Thank the Lord."

As Bart spoke, May took a forward step into view.

"Hello, Mr Turrell." May's face was aglow with her radiant smile, as Bart burst into exclamations of joyful cheers, bringing Mrs Baxter rushing to the door to see what all the commotion was about.

"Well I never," she exclaimed, in a cheery voice, "you must be young May...we've all been praying hard for your safe return...thank the dear Lord for this miracle, now come on in, all of you, this is a just cause for a celebration...now Jack, when was the last time you two young ones ate? I've still got a good helping of lamb hot pot on the stove...and a wonderful apple pie, though I do say so myself, which I baked this afternoon, and I'll fill my largest teapot up. Oh, this is such superb news." Mrs Baxter was still voicing her excitement as she hurried off to the kitchen, demanding they all make themselves at home in her private living quarters. No sooner had they all sat down, when the door knocker was tapping again. Mr

Gascoigne, apologised the minute that Bart pulled the door open, for the lateness of his visit, but, he explained, he'd been taking a late night stroll, and curiosity got the better of him, as he was anxious to find out if there was any news about May.

"Come in Mr Gascoigne, you shouldn't be out on such a treacherous night, you could easily trip up out there."

"Ah, I have my trusty walking stick," declared Mr Gascoigne, waving the wooden stick in the air.

"We're just about to celebrate, Mr Gascoigne. My Jack has rescued our dear May, and they've just this minute arrived home, your timing couldn't have been better, Mr Gascoigne, now do please come in out of the cold. I know Mrs Baxter will be delighted to see you again." Bart had a strong feeling that Mr Gascoigne had taken quite a shine to Mrs Baxter and vice versa.

"Ahh, that's jolly good news, Jolly good. What a young hero your son is, Mr Turrell, you must be proud of him; and how is the young lady, in good health, I trust?"

"Thank God, she appears to be fine, thank you, Mr Gascoigne."

They celebrated well into the early hours of the following morning when Mrs Baxter suddenly declared that Mr Gascoigne couldn't possibly walk back to Windsor Avenue at such a late hour and that since three of her rooms were unoccupied, he could sleep in one of them for the night. She gave May the most feminine room available, which was decorated in pale meadow green wallpaper with vivid wildflowers and tiny colourful birds perched on slim entwined branches. The bed was covered with a sumptuous pastel pink quilted eiderdown, giving the appearance of a fluffy sunset cloud. May was exhausted, and within minutes of her head touching the pillow, she was in a deep sleep.

Bart and Jack continued chatting in low voices as they lay in their beds, both still feeling so moved by all that had happened that sleep had evaded them.

First thing on the following morning Bart and Jack made a trip to the post office to send a telegram home, announcing the safe rescue of May. Although they were still in possession of a healthy sum of money, thanks to Squire Hamilton, they knew that the funds would soon trickle away, and with so many trains and stagecoaches now at a standstill due to the heavy snowfall, which had virtually covered the length and breadth of the country, they knew that it would be a while until they were able to return to Ashley Green; but putting financial problems aside, for the time being, Bart declared that they would worry about that when their pockets were empty. On the journey home, they took a diversion to the busy marketplace and purchased a decent-sized goose and two ducks for Mrs Baxter to cook for Christmas, which was the following day. Jack found a box of fine lace-edged handkerchiefs for May and a heart-shaped tin of sugared almonds.

For Mrs Baxter, they also purchased a large tin of biscuits which was beautifully illustrated with a country scene.

Later that day, Bart, Jack, and May returned to the East End where they attended Tom's funeral; a quiet and rather rushed affair, where at the forefront of everyone's thoughts was the whereabouts of this poor man's murderous brother. As May wiped her tears away, she wondered if Tom had ever seen or felt happiness in his life, or had he just spent it in Bill's shadow; a life of constantly being bullied and ridiculed. May and Edith stood on either side of Martha, supporting her, as she sobbed uncontrollably at Tom's graveside, while the occasional lonely snowflake fluttered down onto the sad and dour day.

Mrs Baxter had insisted that May should invite all of her newly discovered family to spend Christmas day in Paradise Street; she sympathised with the suffering they'd all had to endure, and since all of her lodgers had returned home to their own families for the festive season, she had plenty of empty rooms available. There was nothing Mrs Baxter liked more than to put on a grand spread, and with May's offer of help, she was already revelling in the idea, and eagerly planning the menu and seating arrangements.

CHAPTER TWENTY-FOUR

Eighteen-sixty-one arrived quietly while the country remained shivering under her thick blanket of snow. Temperatures seldom rose above freezing throughout the short winter days, and by night they plummeted, adding more layers of frost and icicles to the brilliantly white and glistening world. The population of London struggled in their difficult battle to keep life running smoothly in the sharp weather, but sadly it was the undertakers who were thriving, with so many deaths, mostly related to the combination of freezing temperatures and poverty.

Bart, Jack, and May were still lodging at Mrs Baxter's warm and comfortable home, where only one of her previous lodgers had managed to return. All three of them were longing to return to Ashley Green and longing for a break in the crippling weather. Even a journey across London to visit Martha, Edith, and Stanley was perilous.

While Bart and Jack ventured out to purchase provisions for Mrs Baxter, May spent her days helping with the housework, cooking and writing letters to Mrs Weaver and the Milton family. She also found time to read her way through a pile of 'penny-dreadful' magazines which she'd found in the broom cupboard. Mrs Baxter insisted that they were left behind by a previous lodger and that she was just keeping them in case he should return to claim them, adding that she couldn't abide the cheaply produced magazines with their unsavoury stories. May tried to conceal her amusement as Mrs Baxter's face became flushed as she quickly changed the subject and began chatting about her renowned fruit cake and how the recipe had been passed down from three generations.

Mr Gascoigne was a frequent visitor, he had arranged with Mrs Baxter to move into one of her vacant rooms when the more favourable weather had returned. They got on exceptionally well together, enjoying each other's company. Mrs Baxter was particularly impressed by his neat and tidy organising skills and was looking forward to him moving in, knowing that he would be bound to help her around the house, keeping everything spick and span.

May was still troubled by the absence of any sightings of Bill. As long as he was free, she felt she'd never completely be able to relax and feel secure. Jack had tried his hardest to convince her that he was no longer a threat to her and that he doubted very much that he would dare to show his face again in these parts, or any place where the police were searching for him, and since he had robbed and attacked Quinton Kingsley, there was now no underhand dealings going on between the pair of them. He added that if Bill had any sense and wanted to escape with his life, he'd probably have left the country by now.

"Please May, you've just got to put him out of your mind, otherwise you'll end up being a nervous wreck," pleaded Jack one afternoon when he'd noticed how uptight May looked.

"It's not only Bill that's worrying me, Jack, it's my half-brother and all this will business. Oh, why couldn't everything be simple, why should he wish me dead? What sort of blood relatives do I have? What with him, and Bill, and Tom…well, I suppose Tom wasn't quite so bad, he was more a victim of circumstance, but it just makes me feel like a lesser person, knowing that I'm related to them."

"May, my dear May, you are the sweetest person I've ever met, and everyone who knows you would say the same. There isn't an ounce of malice or evilness running through your blood. You're a million times better than those rogues.

You heard your aunt and grandmother when they were telling you about your birth mother…Agnes was an angel, just like you are, perhaps not so strong-willed and resolute like you, but you have obviously inherited the finest characteristics from every one of your relatives, plus you were blessed by being nurtured through life by your clever and adoring ma, God bless her soul. So please May, stop thinking so negatively about yourself."

"You're so caring Jack and you always say the kindest words to me. Thank you, I do feel a lot better now, but I won't be happy until that darned will has been read, and we can go home… I miss our lovely green and peaceful world. I miss

Mrs Weaver, Sarah, and little Jenny too. I miss the gentle pace of our life...Oh, Jack; I feel that I must visit Quinton Kingsley, I don't want our first meeting to be in the formal surroundings of the offices of Fenwick, Fenwick, and Montague, where I will be viewed as some money-grabbing nobody. I don't want any of my late father's money at all; it's caused nothing but pain and tragedy so far. Perhaps if I spoke to him first, then he would be able to see me for who I really am. What do you think, Jack?"

As May rose from her chair and went to stand by the window of Mrs Baxter's drawing room, Jack was incredulous at what he was hearing. May really did have the kindest and most forgiving heart.

"May, have you forgotten that this Quinton paid Bill to murder you and your ma." Jack's slightly raised voice was tainted with anger, as he too marched over to the window to stand face-to-face with May. "Unlike Bill and Tom, he knew exactly who you were...he doesn't deserve any sympathy, and definitely no favours from you. He is the cause of all the sorrow and he sits at the root of all evil. I reckon you should have nothing to do with him, and take whatever your late father has bequeathed to you in his will. Besides, I'm sure it will soon be announced, when the reading is to take place, and then you can guarantee that Quinton Kingsley will be up in front of the judge for all of his crimes. I won't be shocked or sorry if he is sent to the gallows, he's a nasty conniving man, who has done some terrible acts, and he's a liar on a grand scale."

As May's eyes glistened with unshed tears, she knew that everything Jack had said was sadly true. It was that small hope somewhere deep in her heart which made her not want to believe that her half-brother could be such a wicked person, and made her wish that she could have a proper relationship with a brother who she hadn't known existed until recently.

"You're absolutely right, Jack, but there is a tiny part of me that wants to believe there is some good in him, and I won't be happy to accept any inheritance until I have had an opportunity to find out for myself what he's really like, and I've got a brilliant idea of how I can safely do it...with your help of course."

Jack didn't like what May was saying. To him, Quinton Kingsley was a dangerous man, and he didn't want May anywhere near him, although he did understand how she wanted to find out for herself, first-hand, what sort of man he was, so he listened intently to what she had planned. Since Quinton was still suffering from his head injury and had been deemed unfit to stand trial, there was a police constable present in his house around the clock, so Jack felt that May would be reasonably safe.

Early the following morning, May and Jack braved the icy conditions and left the house, telling Bart that they were taking a stroll to the nearby park for some fresh air, and to watch the children skating on the frozen pond. As they neared Quinton's house, they took a diversion to a small iron-railed public garden. Inside the park, May handed her thick woollen shawl to Jack and put on a long calico apron, which she had found in Mrs Baxter's linen cupboard, over her navy dress. Jack handed her a folded piece of stiff white card which May carefully pinned into her hair in a semi-circle.

"There," she announced, looking to Jack for approval, "what do you think of nurse Huntley?" Jack wasn't too sure; he didn't have much knowledge of the exact appearance of a nurse's uniform, never having set foot in a hospital, in his life. But, from his vague recollection of pictures he'd seen, he thought that May would pass off as one, especially where she was going.

"You make a fine nurse, May," Jack laughed, "but put your shawl back on, it's freezing."

"I don't think nurses wear woollen shawls, Jack."

"Believe me, May, nobody is gonna point a finger at you just because you're wrapped up warm on such a cold day. You'll look more suspicious walking around as if it's springtime."

"I suppose you're right again, Jack Turrell, come on let's get this done before I get cold feet."

"You mean you haven't got cold feet already," joked Jack, trying to ease May's nerves.

"Oh, you are the funny one...you know what I mean."

Jack pointed out Quinton's house as they neared it, telling her that he would wait out of sight, just on the corner of the street, since everyone in the house might recognise him.

"Should I go in the back way or just knock on the front door, Jack?" questioned May nervously.

"I'm not really sure," said Jack, rubbing the back of his neck, as he tried to come up with an answer, "knock on the front door, May...yes, I don't think that a nurse would use the tradesman's entrance. Be careful May, and good luck,"

"What if the doctor's already there? Jack...that would be dreadful."

"What are the chances? Anyway, Quinton's head is probably fine by now, he's more than likely just playing for time, and making out he's worse than he is. The doctor wouldn't waste his time on him, I'm sure. That's why he sent his nurse to check him over...see...perfect plan, now stop worrying, you'll be fine."

Jack wished that he felt as self-assured as he was trying to sound for May's sake, inside he was quaking at the thought of May going inside Quinton's house.

"I hope you're right, Jack."

Jack quickly kissed May's cheek and watched as she walked the few steps and turned into the Kingsley's house. As May stood nervously waiting for the door to be opened, she kept telling herself to try and look and act positive and confident and not make any silly mistakes. If Quinton was to have any indication as to who she really was, there was no telling what might happen, and she would be in deep water. She could hear the faint sound of footsteps approaching, and as the heavy door was eased open, May thought that this must be the hysterical maid, who Jack had mentioned. She was a young vague looking girl with a very plain face and mousy coloured hair which was tied back in an untidy chignon.

"Yes, can I help yer...Oh, sorry, good morning nurse, have yer come ter see Mr Kingsley?" Since the day Lizzie had encountered the wrath of Bill at the front door she had become a nervous wreck every time, there was a caller. Her voice was tense and high-pitched.

"Good morning, yes, I've been sent by the doctor to check on Mr Kingsley."

"Come in please, nurse," invited Lizzie, "please, just wait 'ere for a minute."

May stood waiting in the impressive hallway feeling strange knowing that she was now in her father's house and that the last time she was here she was a tiny newborn baby, abandoned outside the back entrance. A cold breeze swept through her body, giving her goosebumps.

Lizzie returned, accompanied by a youthful police constable who had obviously just come from the kitchen, with his chin still baring the evidence of a few crumbs. May immediately became more nervous as the policeman walked towards her.

"Good morning, Nurse." As he spoke he took out

a small notebook from his jacket pocket. "Could I 'ave yer name please Miss." Noticing the alarmed expression on May's face, he went on, "nothing to worry about, it's just that in the present circumstances, I 'ave to note down the names of everyone who visits Mr Kingsley."

Feeling slightly calmer, May replied, "Oh, I understand…my name is Lillian Bell."

May stood silently praying that he wasn't going to ask her any more questions and that it wasn't too big of an offence to lie to a policeman. She could feel her heart hammering against her chest and was sure he could hear it too as he jotted down her name.

"Thank you, Nurse Bell," he said, with a slight smile as he replaced his notebook, to the relief of May.

"Lizzie will take you up to see Mr Kingsley; could yer just let me know before yer leave, so I can make a note of the time."

"Of course, I will, thank you, constable," replied May, as she followed Lizzie up the broad sweeping staircase.

CHAPTER TWENTY-FIVE

"Will yer be alright now Miss, only I've got ter go an' 'elp out down in the kitchen, an' Mr Kingsley always shouts at me, so I'd rather not come in with yer." Lizzie stood winding a loose strand of hair around her finger, looking pleadingly at May.

"That's fine...umm, sorry; I don't know your name."

"It's Lizzie, that's short for Elizabeth."

"Well Lizzie, if you could just tell me where I'll be able to find the police constable before I leave here." May wasn't sure who was more nervous, but she could sense that Lizzie found Quinton quite threatening; she'd already turned around, ready to descend back downstairs again.

"Just come down to the kitchen before yer leave, unless yer needs anything, then yer can ring the bell in 'is nib's room," she instructed, nodding her head towards the closed door in front of May, before hurrying away.

May stood for a second to compose herself, feeling uneasy and scared, her hands were shaking, and she could feel the perspiration soaking through her dress. Having a strong urge just to run back down the stairs and out of the front door, she had to remind herself why she was here in her half-brother's house. Taking a deep breath, she knocked on the door. There was no answer, so she turned the handle confidently and walked briskly into the room. The magnitude of Quinton's bedroom shocked her. His enormous four-poster bed looked lost in the centre, as Quinton snored lightly, enclosed by a mass of luxurious pillows, his head barely visible. There was enough fabric in the high ceiling-to-floor curtains to dress every single window in Ashley Green, thought May. On one side of the opulent room stood a large taupe damask chaise lounge, scattered with embroidered cushions. An elaborate crystal chandelier hung from the ceiling, reflecting prisms of light which bounced off every wall and each highly polished piece of furniture. May had never seen such grandeur in her life, she had thought that Mrs Baxter's bedrooms were extravagant, but this was the sort of bedroom she would imagine Queen Victoria to have in the palace.

As she painstakingly walked across the huge detailed oriental rug, she tried to imagine what a real nurse would do in such a situation, nerves were getting the better of her, and just as she was about to make an about-turn and make a speedy exit, Quinton pulled himself up, moaning in a mumbled voice about having no privacy in his own home. He stared at May as if his brain was trying to register why there was a nurse hovering over him. May could do nothing but freeze, as her mouth fell open and seemed to dry up at the same time as all the words evaporated from her head. In the awkward atmosphere, it was Quinton who spoke first, and he was far from pleased.

"Who in the blazes let you into my room, unannounced? Who are you?" His voice was harsh, and his staring cold eyes appeared soulless. May struggled as she tried to remember her alias name, but failed as Quinton's eyes continued to bore into her, making her feel more uncomfortable with every slow second which passed.

"I'm a nurse," she suddenly blurted out, thinking how ridiculous and unprofessional she sounded. "The doctor asked me to call on you to see how you are fairing, Mr Kingsley...so er, how is your health today?"

Quinton became flushed and pink-faced as he hauled his overweight body up into a sitting position. His bandage was slack and had slipped down to one side of his round head. His long drooping moustache didn't suit his flabby face, thought May, and his neck was invisible beneath his double chin.

"Well, do what you have to do nurse, and get a move on, I haven't even been given breakfast yet."

May took a step closer, reaching out to touch the unravelling bandage.

"I think this old thing needs some attention,"

May said, convincingly, "so I'll just put it right for you. I hope you're not in too much pain, Mr Kingsley?"

"Just get on with it girl, the only thing that's in pain is my stomach, the head's fine."

"Well, let me take a look...how did this happen, Mr

Kingsley?"

Giving May a stern glare, Quinton continued,

"I was attacked with a poker and robbed in my own home…and when you are a pillar of society like myself, that is the very last thing you expect to happen."

May took her time in replacing the bandage, wanting to listen more to what Quinton had to say for himself.

"That's terrible," May sympathised, "were you alone in the house when it happened?"

As May studied Quinton's head, seeing only a small lump and a healing scab, Quinton didn't answer her question but seemed deep in thought about something.

"It's looking very well, Mr Kingsley…healing up nicely."

"I dare say you noticed the presence of a police constable downstairs nurse…er…do you have a name?"

"Oh yes, of course, I do, it's Lillian Bell," stated May, with relief that the name had come back to her.

"Well, Nurse Bell, the police think that I'm behind a plot to murder my illegitimate half-

sister, who I have never even met. Can you believe such a ridiculous notion? They also believe that I was behind the murder of her mother, who I believe, lost her life in a house fire some two hundred miles away, which of course is absolute balderdash. The loathsome thug, who did this to me, has framed me, telling everyone that I was the organiser of such a horrendous crime, and, is probably intent on blackmailing me too."

"That's terrible," sympathised May, trying her best to sound genuine. "But, I don't understand, why would this person make such an accusation…and surely the police wouldn't possibly find any truth in it." May tugged on the bell pull hoping that Lizzie would soon appear. "I think it's high time you were given your breakfast Mr Kingsley."

Minutes later, a knock on the door was followed by the entrance of an awkward-looking Lizzie, who stood waiting for her orders.

"Did you ring, Sir?" Quinton ignored her, continuing to gawk at May, who had decided to issue her request.

"Hello Lizzie, Mr Kingsley would like his breakfast, please."

"Yes, Nurse."

After a half curtsy, she disappeared quickly through the door again.

"Ridiculous little thing," Quinton moaned. "Can't understand why Mrs Booth recommended such a half-wit of a girl."

"You'll feel better once you've eaten, and if you've done nothing wrong, then you should have nothing to fear. I'm sure the police don't go around locking up innocent people."

"I hope you're right, Nurse Bell, but the death of the damned girl's mother is looking like a sticking point."

May felt a sudden torment, on hearing her beloved

ma mentioned in such a disrespectful manner, and at the same time as being in such proximity to the instigator.

"That's very sad indeed, what of her daughter, your half-sister? She must be suffering a great deal. I imagine a pillar of society like yourself, you must be desperate to meet and help her."

Quinton looked shocked that this nurse should be so concerned about the welfare of his half-sister. To him, she was the cause of all his problems, and he couldn't care less about her.

"Er...yes, quite true, though I heard that she was brought up in some far-off farming county community, and has grown up to be a simple, uneducated peasant girl, who's really not worth worrying about, and certainly wouldn't know what to do with any sum of money that my late father might have bequeathed to her...though God knows why I can't possibly comprehend. Probably would have done her a favour if she had died alongside her mother...would have done me a favour, I can tell you. I truly believe that the poor peasants of this land would not benefit from riches. It would totally confuse and destroy them... I mean, they thrive on working in all those menial jobs. No, in fact, it would be a cruel punishment by my father to leave anything more than a few pounds to that waif."

Thankfully, a gentle knock on the door bringing Lizzie in with a full tray of breakfast, served as a reminder to May that she had to keep calm no matter what poison spilt out from her half-brother's mouth. Minute by minute, she was growing to detest him more than she had imagined possible. She had heard more than enough. Quinton Kingsley was no more than a pompous leech, and she felt ashamed and saddened that there was a blood tie between them.

"About time!" Quinton yelled, almost making poor Lizzie drop the whole load as she placed the tray onto the small bed table with unsteady hands. "As soon as I'm up and about again, there's going to be some major changes under my roof."

"Thank you, Sir. Will that be all?"

"Get out!" Quinton bellowed, his face bright red, as sweat, dripped from his brow. Turning his attention to May, he said, "I don't suppose you would be interested in a post in my house? I would top your nurse's pay, and there would definitely be some perks if you take good care of me... think about it, Nurse Bell, I doubt that you will ever receive another such generous offer to match mine."

May could feel the bile in the back of her throat, her whole body was tense, and there were a string of sentences that she wished she could hurl at this thick-skinned, spoilt, snob of a man, whose attitude towards anyone in unfortunate circumstances was utterly repugnant.

"I can't think of anywhere worse than being in the firing line of your verbal onslaughts, Mr Kingsley. It would be a desperate measure to work for anyone as arrogant and pig-headed as you, so on those grounds, I will have to decline your offer."

Not hearing the response that he was expecting, Quinton was unable to speak. His mouth had fallen open in shock, and that's how he remained as May turned around and paced out of his bedroom, and out through the front door, not bothering to report her departure to the constable. By the time she had run down the few stone steps leading from Quinton's house, her eyes were blinded by tears. She couldn't get away quick enough and fled as fast as her shaking legs would carry her to the corner of the street, where Jack was standing anxiously waiting. As she fell into Jack's arms, he wished that he'd tried to stop May from visiting Quinton, he'd had a feeling it would be a disaster.

"He didn't harm you, did he," demanded Jack, defensively.

"That ...that...thing, is not human, and if he has a heart, which I doubt, it has gone rusty and black, far beyond repair," exclaimed May, in between sobs of anger and sorrow.

CHAPTER TWENTY-SIX

Three weeks had passed since May's upsetting ordeal with Quinton Kingsley. The snow had finally cleared, and although movement around London and everybody's daily lives became easier, the East End slums once again looked dull and foreboding with the disappearance of her bright and sparkling mask. Martha was slowly getting over the loss of Tom and was still living with Edith and Stanley. Much to Mrs Baxter's delight, Mr Gascoigne had moved into one of her vacant rooms; she was busy fussing over him, making sure his blankets were adequate, and that he found the room warm and big enough, and numerous other enquiries, enough to make him want to move out again just for some peace and quiet, thought Bart, Jack, and May as they watched her with amusement.

There was still no sign of Bill, which was proving to be the biggest worry for everyone, especially Martha, who was convinced that her son had gone completely mad and was now capable of anything, even as far as murdering his own mother. May spent as much of her time as she could in the company of her newly discovered family, and was trying her hardest to convince them all to leave London and join her in Cheshire. They also suggested that she should remain in London, close to them, since they were now a family and had so much lost time to make up, and emphasised how many more opportunities there were in the City. May though, could only see London as dirty, overcrowded, and far too noisy. She was sure that if they just spent a few days in the glorious countryside of Cheshire, with all its clean air and wide open spaces, they would be reluctant to return to London. May was sure that her grandfather's delicious pies would be as much in demand in Chester as they were in London, and he would be able to make a good living there. May thought it would also be beneficial for the whole family to move away from the bad memories of all the tragedies which had occurred to them in London.

Quinton Kingsley had been certified healthy enough to be thoroughly interrogated by Sergeant Rawlins down at the police station, but with the lack of hard evidence, and with the absence of Bill Haines, there was no proof of any crime committed to charge him with, so Sergeant Rawlins, reluctantly had no other choice than to release him, even though he thought him very capable of committing all the crimes which he had been accused of. He would be keeping a watchful eye on him in the future, and as soon as they had caught Bill, he was confident that Quinton would become unstuck.

To the great relief of George Fenwick, a date

had finally been set, in five days, for the hearing of Sir Jeremiah Kingsley's will. It would be like shedding a heavy load, he thought, to be able to finally close the Kingsley file. He had made a firm decision not to have any further business with Quinton Kingsley once the will had eventually been finalised. He had taken a strong dislike to this man and didn't trust him.

It was in London's Victoria Park where Jack bent on one knee and delivered his proposal of marriage to May, which she happily accepted. He had decided to propose to her before the reading of the will, just in case people took to thinking that he was marrying her for her inheritance, which was far from the truth, not that he thought she was going to be left a fortune, more likely to be a modest token amount. Ideally, Jack would have preferred to wait till they were amongst the familiar surroundings of Ashley Green, a place close to both of their hearts and that they missed terribly. The weather on that day had been cold and crisp, with the sun shining cheerfully in the cloudless azure sky. Jack had bought a silver and white opal filigree engagement ring for May telling her that when they returned home she would have his mother's expensive gold and diamond ring. May had stressed though, that since this was the ring he had placed on her finger, she would never take it off again, and to her, it was worth more than the crown jewels. May held the small posy of dried carnations, African violets, and lavender which Jack had given her, as they strolled, arm in arm through Victoria Park; they felt like the happiest couple in the world. Jack excitedly spoke of his plans for the following months leading up to the day when they would become husband and wife. He was eager to start his new job at Squire Hamilton's estate, and save as much money as he could; he told May of how he intended to be a good husband, and provide for her every need. Jack was hoping that after the great transformation of his landscape garden, the Squire would keep him on as a permanent gardener. May had decided that she would continue to work for Sarah Milton, provided that she still wanted her. She was also eager to tell her about some exciting ideas that she'd had regarding her dressmaking business.

When Jack and May arrived back in Paradise Street, they found a welcoming party and a spread of food which Mrs Baxter had laid on to celebrate their engagement. Edith and Stanley were jubilant that their granddaughter was to marry Jack who they had grown to love over the past few weeks, they could see how much Jack adored May and knew that she would always be safe with this caring, sensible young man.

Martha was already planning everyone's wedding outfits, and feeling angry that she had lost all her beautiful, elaborate garments in the fire, most of which had been given to her over the years by her eccentric friends who were involved in the theatre. Bart was also euphoric, and couldn't wish for a lovelier daughter-in-law, he was thrilled that at long last there was a happy event to celebrate, and prayed that eighteen-sixty-one would continue to be a good year for them all, after such a disastrous previous year.

The day of the reading of the will arrived. Quinton's eyes nearly popped out of his head when he caught sight of May as she entered the offices of Fenwick, Fenwick, and Montague, with Mr Gascoigne.

"*You!*" declared Quinton, rising from his chair, his face taut with rage.

"Is there a problem, Mr Kingsley?" enquired Mr Fenwick, as he acknowledged May. Quinton didn't reply. "Have you had the pleasure of meeting your half-sister yet, Mr Kingsley?"

"No, but I did have the pleasure of meeting Nurse Bell," replied Quinton, sarcastically. Mr Fenwick gave him a puzzled look, thinking that maybe he hadn't quite recovered from his recent head injury. "Please, Miss Huntley, do take a seat. Mr Gascoigne, if you could sit on this side of the room next to Mrs Booth," he requested, shaking his hand firmly. May was seated on the opposite side from Mr Gascoigne, and on the same side as Quinton. In front of the small assembly, Mr Fenwick sat rather stiffly behind his sparse desk, on which lay the last will and testament of Sir Jeremiah Kingsley. Quinton's body seemed to fill most of the pokey office, as he sat arrogantly with his chest puffed out, glaring down at the beneficiaries as if they had no right to be there. May was unable to look at him. Remembering the harsh and cruel words which he had spoken to her on their last meeting, she kept her eyes lowered.

Once they were all seated, Mr Fenwick greeted them all with a quick smile as he prepared to deliver what he viewed to be one of the most enlightening wills that he'd seen in some time. He was looking forward to seeing the reactions of a couple of the beneficiaries.

After the formalities and the legal jargon, George Fenwick announced that his client had specifically instructed him to read out this next statement. He began;

"My dear associates and loved ones, firstly, let me express my sincere gratitude to you all for attending this reading of my will. There will be a few shocks, and I wish to explain to those concerned, my reasons for the way I have divided my estate. I wish to express my sincere gratitude to Mrs Charlotte Booth, and Mr Arthur Gascoigne, who have been my most trusted, loyal, and reliable staff throughout my life. I thank you for your devoted service. I am beholden to Mrs Emma Huntley, a fine selfless young woman, who sacrificed her life to raise and care for my daughter. Regrettably, I have never shown my appreciation to her in words, but, I hope my bequest to her will

express how I am forever indebted to her."

As Mrs Booth and Mr Gascoigne exchanged smiles, both pleased that their years of devoted service had been recognised and appreciated, May shuffled slightly in her chair, trying hard to hold back her tears. She really didn't want to break down in Mr Fenwick's office, especially with Quinton Kingsley sat glaring at her. Mr Fenwick continued;

"There is only one of my beneficiaries who I feel that I must apologise to; my dear daughter, May Huntley, whose beautiful late mother meant so much to me, and who I adored with all of my heart and soul. We have not been fortunate enough to of had the kind of relationship that every father and daughter should share, due to circumstances beyond my control. I hope that my bequest to you, my dear daughter, will make up a little for any hardships which you have had to endure in your life and enable you to have a comfortable future.
Be happy, May, and please, try to forgive me."

There was little that May could do to stop her tears from falling. She wished that Jack was with her, and could sense Quinton's angry eyes boring into her. Mrs Booth surreptitiously wiped her tears away with her handkerchief. She remembered clearly the day that Jeremiah's tiny scrap of a baby was screaming in her kitchen. In her mourning, poor Emma had felt the overwhelming need to comfort and suckle that baby. They were two poor abandoned souls, united together.

Mr Fenwick took a sip of water, and continued;

"Finally, to my dear son, Quinton, who has given me much pleasure over the years, but however, has yet to prove himself in this world, and has been unable to financially support himself, and has shown no inclination whatsoever to earn his own living. If you wish to continue living in the style and manner to which you have been accustomed, then you will have to make an honest living. I wish you every success in your future business, son, and sincerely hope that you find happiness and purpose in your life.
Be kind to others, and remember to be truthful and honest in all that you do."

Silence filled the now stuffy office. Jeremiah Kingsley had given everybody something to think about. For the first time in her life, May felt a kind of connection to her father and regretted not ever having had the opportunity to meet him. He sounded caring and kind and he had obviously loved her birth mother very much, although she would keep these opinions to herself, knowing how her grandparents and Aunty Martha felt about him. He was also, it seemed, able to see through his son, and by the sound of it, knew exactly what he was like.

Mr Fenwick coughed loudly,

"Right, ladies and gentlemen, if you would all compose yourselves, I shall press on." He noticed the embarrassment on Quinton's red face as he sat twiddling with his pocket watch.

"After all existing debts, funeral expenses, and outstanding payment of bills have been settled, my estate shall be divided accordingly. To my employees, Charlotte

Booth, and Arthur Gascoigne, I bequeath the sum of one hundred pounds each. To Emma Huntley, I bequeath the sum of two hundred pounds. Should the beneficiary be deceased then the bequest is to be given to May Huntley. To May Huntley, I bequeath the sum of five thousand pounds. Five hundred pounds, to be paid immediately, and four thousand five hundred pounds to be held in a trust until she attains the age of twenty-one years."

As loud gasps reverberated around the office, May sat in shock at what she had heard. Quinton, who was unable to contain his anger, pushed his chair back violently as he stood up, his arms in the air, and his mouth about to start firing a string of abuse. Mr Fenwick left his seat hastily, commanding Quinton to sit back down and control himself while he completed the reading of the will. Silence again resumed as Mr Fenwick continued, his voice an octave higher.

"Should the beneficiary be deceased, then the bequest is to be divided equally between her four nearest living relatives, with the exemption of Quinton Kingsley."

George Fenwick stopped for a brief moment, peering over the top of his spectacles at Quinton, as he issued yet another stern warning look.

"And finally, to my son, Quinton Kingsley, I bequeath the sum of fifty pounds and my total real estate, namely, twenty-five Wilton Place, Belgravia, London, along with all furniture. Should the beneficiary be deceased, the bequest is to be given to May Huntley."

George Fenwick folded the will slowly, and replaced it into its large brown envelope.

CHAPTER TWENTY-SEVEN

"Come on now, hurry up before we miss the train," Bart pleaded, as May hugged and kissed everyone goodbye for the third time.

"Now remember, you promised me that you will come to Ashley Green when me and Jack get wed," May reminded them all in a croaky voice, as her eyes filled with tears. Edith handed her a handkerchief, reassuring her that nothing in the world would keep them away.

"We've lived over seventeen years, always thinking about you, and wondering where you were, what you looked like, and if we would ever see you again. Rest assured, you'll never be out of our lives, as long as we breathe air, now just you remember that, May. We love you dearly, and you're now part of our lives forevermore. Now off you go before we all run out of hankies." Edith wiped away her tears with the flat of her hand before giving May a final hug.

The train station was noisy and extremely busy. Bart was fast becoming impatient, and fretful that they might miss the train, especially since there wouldn't be another until the following day, and he didn't dare think about having to go through all those 'goodbyes' again.

"Let them board the train now," commanded Stanley, knowing that the womenfolk were finding it difficult to wrench themselves away from May. "It won't be long till we are all united again, you know how time just flies by."

May watched as her new family made their way towards the station exit. After every few steps, Edith and Martha would turn around to wave until they were eventually out of sight. Letting out a deep sigh as she dried her face with the damp handkerchief, May held on tightly to Jack's arm as they hurriedly followed Bart's footsteps towards the waiting train.

The journey was long and tiring, and it was late evening before they arrived in Chester, all of them feeling weary, and aching from being seated for such a long period. May had suggested that they should spend the night in a hotel in Chester so they would arrive home refreshed and during daylight hours on the following morning. There were also a few shops which May wanted to visit before the final leg of the journey. As anxious as they were to reach their cottage, Bart and Jack were too tired to disagree with May's suggestion, so without wasting any more time, they booked into the Queen's Hotel in the heart of the City.

"What exactly do you want to buy in town, May," enquired Jack, as they sat in the hotel dining room at breakfast the following morning. "You hardly left anything behind from those shopping trips in London, you've enough fabric, buttons, ribbons and lace to make dresses for all the women in Cheshire already," stated Jack, as he tucked into his plate of eggs and devilled kidneys.

"Oh don't exaggerate, Jack, if Mrs Milton likes the sound of my idea, which I'm sure she will, the supplies which I purchased in London will soon run out, anyway, I don't intend to buy more supplies today, no, it's something much more exciting. Just you wait and see," she said teasingly. Jack was intrigued.

"Jack, do you think that the pawn shop I was telling you about, near the station, will still have my ma's silver necklace? I would love to be able to retrieve it, but it's been such a long time since Bill pawned it, I'm sure somebody would have bought it by now; it's such a pretty piece of jewellery. Is it worth asking, do you think?"

"I'll visit the pawn shop an' ask for yer, while you an' Jack go an' do yer shopping," volunteered Bart.

"Thank you, Mr Turrell, that would be really helpful, and save us time."

"An' yer gonna 'ave to stop calling me Mr Turrell, May, we're practically family...how about Uncle Bart?"

May gently patted her mouth with her napkin, and fluttered her dark eyelashes, something she'd witnessed the other women doing in the dining room.

"Uncle Bart it is then, but it will take a while to get used to, since all my life you have been Mr Turrell. I might not always get it right."

Bart and Jack both laughed, finding the way that May was imitating the wealthy Ladies in the room amusing.

Bart stood outside the pawn shop searching the window. There was a vast display of eye-catching necklaces, sparkling brooches and cameos, gemstone set rings, and many other jewellery items, but there was no sign of the pretty silver pendant and chain that for so many years he'd seen decorating Emma's neck. He was as anxious to reclaim it as much as May. It was part of Emma, a gift from her late grandmother, and a reminder to Bart of the woman he had loved deeply for many years. It now rightfully belonged on her daughter's neck, and it angered him that Bill had tainted it with his filthy hands. Bart decided to enter the shop and enquire about it, nothing would be lost, he thought.

As he began to describe the necklace, giving the pawnbroker the distinctive description of Bill, Bart listened intently, hearing how the pawnbroker had been particularly suspicious of Bill. Telling Bart how he had noticed the rough way in which he'd handled May and the distressing look on her tearful face. He had kept the necklace safely in his drawer and was happy to sell it back to him, and even happier to hear that May was now safe. As they chatted away, Bart told him part of how May had come to be with Bill and Tom that day, warning him about how dangerous a man Bill was, and now a wanted man, just in case he should happen to show up again in these parts. The pawnbroker went on to tell Bart how he had rescued the poor horse and cart that they'd abandoned opposite his shop. He took pity on the starving animal and brought him into his backyard to take care of him. Bart couldn't believe his luck; he had given up all hope of ever setting his eyes on Chestnut again. The pawnbroker was glad that at last, the horse was to be united with his rightful owner, and even though Bart insisted on paying him for all of his troubles, the pawnbroker refused to accept a single penny. Bart left the shop a happier man and pleased that they could now travel back to Ashley Green in his horse and cart.

May had finally purchased her mystery item, a very technical and impressive-looking, 'Chadwick and Jones' hand sewing machine, which came in its own protective wooden box with a handle, ideal for Jack who had to carry the heavy load back to the hotel. She also couldn't resist buying a wooden hobby horse for Jenny and a set of colourful alphabet blocks for baby Adam.

It was late morning before they arrived in Ashley Green. Although the weather was chilly and wet, nothing could dampen Bart and Jack's spirits as they neared their cottage. May, however, was experiencing mixed feelings. She had gained so much knowledge of her family history over the past weeks. So much had happened to her in such a short period of time that it was causing her emotions to be in a state of uncertainty. She was experiencing flashbacks of the days when she and her ma lived contently in their snug cottage before she had known the truth about her ancestry. The cottage remained in its same gloomy state of disrepair as when she'd last seen it; as if it had died along with her ma and was a distressing reminder of that dreadful night back in November. She wasn't sure if Mrs Weaver had yet returned to her own cottage or if she was still staying on the Milton's farm.

She was wealthy but had no home to call her own, and she was in the only place that had ever been home to her, but today she felt oddly out of place. After waiting excitedly for such a long time for this homecoming, she now felt downhearted.

"What's wrong, May?" questioned Jack, noticing how quiet and withdrawn she'd become.

"I have no home, Jack. I've just realised, and I feel suddenly out of place."

"Come on May, your home is gonna be with me soon. Besides, you've lived here all of your life...how else could I call you my darling May of Ashley Green? I know it must be upsetting for you to arrive back here and see your old cottage in such a sorry state, but things will soon change, you'll see. We'll get wed in the spring, and then our home will be together, May. We'll live in the sweetest cottage in all of Cheshire, and we'll be the happiest couple. You just wait and see."

Many of their neighbours had appeared out of their homes to welcome the return of Bart, Jack, and May, especially May, whose disappearance had caused so much worry in Ashley Green. As Bart and Jack unloaded the horse cart, the womenfolk all greeted May with warm embraces. They also presented them with a freshly baked batch of hot scones and a cottage loaf.

"You see," declared Jack, "there's no welcome like that in London, is there."

As Jack ushered May inside, she declared,

"Oh...just ignore me, Jack. I'm being silly and too sentimental. I should be grateful that I have such wonderful, caring friends, neighbours, and family, not to mention an incredible fiancé, who risked his life to rescue me. What would Ma say if she were alive? She would admonish me, and tell me to count my blessings and to remember all of those poor souls who are far worse off than me."

"Exactly," agreed Jack, "now, let's try and find somewhere to store all of your shopping. I think we might need a larger cottage...how much did you buy, May!"

"Well it's not all for me, Jack, and I told you, most of it is for my business idea. Just wait till I tell Mrs Milton, she's going to be over the moon, and she is the one woman who thoroughly deserves some happiness, not forgetting dear Mrs Weaver of course, who is kindness itself."

"There you see, you're feeling better already."

Jack took May's hand in his as he gently pulled her towards him, wrapping his arms around her petite frame as he tenderly kissed her lips.

"My sweet May, please don't ever be sad my love."

The mood was broken as Bart, returned with the heavy sewing machine from the cart, coughing loudly before stepping over the threshold to the cottage.

"What on earth is in this box? Yer didn't bring a pile of those London bricks home for a keepsake, did yer May?"

"It's a sewing machine, Pa," announced Jack, breaking away from a blushing May.

"So what's wrong with good old fashioned 'and sewing? It's a far quicker an' safer way of making yer clothes."

"May's hoping to start a proper dressmaking business with Mrs Milton, Pa, so they're gonna need a proper machine for that."

"Possibly two or more machines once our beautiful gowns are in great demand by all the wealthy ladies of Cheshire," added May.

Bart was looking slightly puzzled as he stood the machine on the table giving it a curious glance.

"That's all very well, but where's the hot tea that I was promised ter go with them lovely fresh scones that 'ave been teasing me nostrils since we arrived 'ome," he asked jokingly.

Feeling a lot happier now, and realising how much she was loved, May set to brew the tea, making herself at home in the kitchen, with a warm optimistic sentiment that the future was looking bright and promising.

EPILOGUE

It couldn't have been a more beautiful day, and the weather more obliging, than on the twenty-first of May in eighteen-sixty-one, when May and Jack were married. Edith, Stanley, Martha, Mrs Baxter, and Mr Gascoigne had all arrived in Cheshire to be part of this special day. Everyone was in high spirits and delighted to witness the happy young couple become husband and wife. On this unseasonably hot and sunny day with just a light gentle breeze in the air, a grand banquet was held in the lower meadow, amongst the wild scarlet poppies, yellow cowslips, and blue cornflowers of the Milton's farm, where Stan Milton had constructed a sizable lengthy table with seating benches either side of it. The table was covered with a huge brilliant white damask cotton tablecloth, on top of which laid a generous spread, eagerly prepared by the womenfolk of Ashley Green, along with three dozen of Stanley's finest meat pies, and a stunning wedding cake, skilfully baked and elaborately decorated by Betty from Hamilton house.

Squire Hamilton had generously presented the couple with a delightful cottage on his estate for them to live in while Jack continued in his employment, saying jokingly, that it was mostly for his benefit to make sure that Jack wouldn't be late for work in the mornings.

Little Jenny Milton had been in awe of her idol and pestered Sarah every day after the wedding as to when she would be able to get married and wear a beautiful, flowing dress as May had worn. It was a day to remember, and a day that May would keep safely locked in her heart to treasure for the rest of her life.

May and Sarah's dressmaking business was flourishing. Sarah had been overjoyed to receive such a wonderful gift of a sewing machine from May. She had never thought that she would own one in her lifetime. She was also thrilled at the copious, beautiful and varied fabric which May had purchased in London. The early days proved to be exceedingly hectic, with barely any chance for a respite. The kitchen at Milton farm was transformed into what looked more like a workshop; the sewing machine took centre stage on the table, and every inch of spare worktop was covered with all the dressmaking paraphernalia. Baby Adam, who thankfully was very well behaved, provided he had a full tummy, sat in his small wooden high chair observing with interest as May and Sarah worked around the clock to produce their elegant gowns. They joked that Adam would probably grow up to be a tailor with all the early influence he was subjected to. Jenny had become quite the expert, giving her advice as to which ribbons, lace, and buttons should be matched to each different fabric, more than often sending Sarah and May into fits of laughter at her bizarre choices. With the help of Bart, Stan set to work converting the outbuilding, where Bill and Tom had spent their days, into a workshop. Although Sarah and May were quite sceptical about the idea, Stan had merely told them to wait until they had seen the finished project before making their decision.

Within four weeks the building was completely transformed. Six large holes had been knocked into the walls and fitted with windows, allowing the natural light to flood into the room, and providing a delightful scenic view of the rolling fields on one side, and full vision of the farmhouse on the other. Long high worktops stretched along two of the walls beneath the windows, with plenty of storage space and drawers in between each high-backed padded stool. A spacious cupboard stood against the third wall, for hanging the completed dresses, and along the fourth wall, Bart had constructed an impressive fireplace. The days of this cold, dark and musty-smelling store room had now gone, hopefully, prayed Stan, along with its ugly memories. Stan had even built another high chair for Adam, and, he had said, for any other baby who might be in need of a seat in the future.

Sarah and May were delighted with the building, and couldn't believe what an amazing job Stan and Bart had done. Within a few hours, the farmhouse kitchen had been restored to normality, and their new sewing room was in full swing. May had ordered another sewing machine, and shortly after her and Jack's wedding, they took on a young girl from Ashley Green to sew all the simple straight seams.

Within eighteen months, the business was thriving, and they now sold most of their dresses and accessories to an exclusive ladies' clothes shop in Chester which was called Martha and Edith's Fine Ladies Fashion and was next door to Stanley's Traditional London Pies. May had persuaded them to move up to Cheshire, shortly after she had given birth to baby William in the autumn of sixty-two, a beautiful healthy boy, and the apple of his parent's eyes. They were initially renting the premises along with the living accommodation above until May turned twenty-one when after accessing her inheritance, she intended to buy them as a special gift for her loving family, and a sound investment.

Although at first, Martha, Edith and Stanley were reluctant to make the life-changing move from London; the compromise was that they live in the bustling town of Chester where they felt more at home, as opposed to the contrasting quiet countryside of Ashley Green and its surrounds. Stanley's pie shop had, as May had predicted, had become one of the most popular food shops of its kind in Chester. Stanley had also set up a few tables where the patrons could sit and eat their pie and mash inside the shop. Mrs Weaver had also become involved, giving her a whole new lease on life. She had never been so busy, making miniature fruit pies which went down a treat in Stanley's pie shop. In the evenings she would busy herself knitting clothes for baby William, and all the unborn babies which she was convinced would one day fill Jack and May's happy home, telling May that she was just making hay while the sun shone and that one day her eyesight would not allow her to continue with her knitting.

Jack continued to work for the Squire, even though the landscape garden had been completed. He had become a very knowledgeable gardener over the months, and now continued working to maintain the expansive grounds on Cedric Hamilton's estate until the future plan of purchasing the farm adjacent to the Milton's farm, could take place when May's inheritance was accessible.

Bart Turrell was now working on Stan Milton's farm. They had become good friends over the months and with Bart undertaking all the tasks which Stan wasn't able to do because of his disability, the running of the farm had improved immensely, and was, at last, making a profit. May had also bought Stan a gift of a small flock of sheep to add to the farm.

Mr Gascoigne continued to lodge with Mrs Baxter in Paradise Street. Every six months or so, they would travel up to Cheshire. May was working hard trying to convince them both to make a permanent move to the area. Although Arthur Gascoigne was keen, Mrs Baxter still needed a bit more persuading.

Quinton Kingsley had returned to his home after the reading of his father's will and immediately fired Mrs Booth and Lizzie without their final week's pay, and without giving them any notice. Lizzie couldn't leave quick enough and returned to her large family in the East End. Mrs Booth decided it was high time that she retired from service, and arranged to live with her widowed sister in Worthing.

Spending the first few months behind drawn curtains, and living amongst his daily mess and squalor, Quinton felt betrayed by his own father and wracked his brains as to why he had been treated so harshly and unfairly. With no money and no income, he began selling items of value from his family home. From the solid silver trays and cutlery, and his late mother's jewellery, to pieces of antique furniture and heirlooms. He had lost all sense of self-respect, becoming rude and abusive in all of his dealings, and earning himself a bad reputation. Becoming lost in his spacious Belgravia home, which was fast being emptied, room by room, Quinton gambled the money away from every sale, eager to make the fortune that he felt he had been robbed of, but never succeeding. It was during a dispute with one of the dealers who Quinton believed was drastically undervaluing a silver antique trinket box that he came up with the idea of opening his own antique shop.

Within six months he had sold the family home, and purchased a considerably smaller townhouse along with a substantial-sized shop which was soon well stocked and attracting a lot of interest. Quinton, it seemed, had finally found a way of making a living, and was revelling in his new occupation. His newfound passion for antiques had transformed his whole outlook on life; he had become polite, courteous, and extremely diligent. His appearance took on a whole new stylish look, and he had slimmed down to half the man he used to be.

The whereabouts of Bill was never far from anyone's thoughts. May often suffered horrendous nightmares, where, if Bill wasn't dragging her brutally off to a gloomy desolate place, he was kidnapping baby William. As happy and contented as May was, it was Bill who still continued to put a black mark on her life, robbing her of peace of mind, and haunting her nights.

In November of eighteen-sixty-three, during one of May's regular visits to Edith and Martha's shop, she found Martha in a terrible distraught state. She was distressed, that after nearly three years, she'd received a letter all the way from America, from Bill, which had been forwarded to her from the occupants of her previous home in the East End. He gave no forwarding address, nor mentioned which part of the country he was living in. His letter merely stated that he would never be returning home since he knew that the gallows awaited him. He enquired about nobody and failed to write an apology for any of the unforgivable deeds which he had committed, showing no remorse or guilt. It upset Martha immensely, serving as a reminder of how cold and callous Bill had become. She harboured the sweet memories in her heart of his much younger days, when he had been one of the cutest little boys in the neighbourhood, with a permanent smile upon his cheery face, and would go out of his way to please his mother. May and Edith tried their hardest to comfort her, saying that it was because Bill was feeling so guilty that he was unable to ask about the well-being of his family, and it was through his guilt that he had felt the need to write, and how it proved he was thinking about her. To May, though, it was the biggest blessing she could have wished for, just to know that there were thousands of miles and an ocean between Bill and her precious family meant that she would now sleep peacefully and enjoy her new family life.

Peaseblossom had truly found Heaven in the

bountiful grounds of Squire Hamilton's estate which were a far cry from the harsh and inhospitable streets of the East End. She had grown into a plump and spoilt cat, spending her days either exploring every corner of her newfound domain or lazing by the fireside in May and Jack's cottage, unless baby William was crying, then she would make a quick dive under the bed.

Dear Reader, I hope you have enjoyed reading this book; if you have, please consider leaving a review. It will be greatly appreciated and really does make a difference. Thank you, Lilly Adam.

ABOUT THE AUTHOR

Lilly Adam

Lilly Adam was born in London where she spent her early childhood. From a young age, she always had a passion for reading, writing stories and poetry. With maturity her interest in history blossomed, especially for the Victorian era; it was a period in history that saw so much change and an abundance of new and life-changing inventions and laws, making it such an interesting era to study. With a lifelong ambition to become an author, it was after a long pause whilst raising her family in Oxfordshire, that she finally found the time to put pen to paper and begin. Her debut novel, May of Ashley Green was published in February 2017. She has since published a further thirteen novels and continues to write. Turning her passion into a fulfilling career as a professional author has proved a most rewarding achievement.

My strong passion for writing and keen interest in history, especially the Victorian Era, has influenced me to engage wholeheartedly in writing historical fiction/romance/mystery. I love engaging with the projects I work on, diving headfirst into the research, investigation, and production of stories that I feel are worth writing about, and will prove entertaining to an audience intrigued by this genre. I am a dedicated writer and aim to preserve as much authenticity as possible when delving into the past.

BOOKS BY THIS AUTHOR

Stella

Set at the end of the nineteenth century, a gripping story of Stella, a beautiful young woman in her twenties. Already the Lady of the grand Sunny Meadow House on the outskirts of Oxford, due to her marriage to the wealthy and much senior James Headly, when James suddenly becomes bankrupt Stella is faced with some devastating changes in her life.

During a journey to London in search of work, James is set upon, robbed and left for dead. Taking advantage of James's loss of memory, the evil Claudia Wiggins, sets out to achieve her lifelong dream. Stella's discovery that she is with child, shortly before learning that she is a widow, makes her determined to find a way to financially support herself and her unborn child. With the help of Hetty, Stella's former maid, Glorious Bakes is opened in Oxford's High Street, but life for Stella is never without its traumas and complications.

Poppy Woods

When Lady Margaret Hutchinson abandons her illegitimate daughter in 1863 she does not foresee the consequences of her actions. Set in Victorian Oxfordshire the story of Poppy Woods tells of a courageous girl, who from her very first breath suffers neglect and cruelty. Illegally Adopted by the tight fisted and merciless Sidney Woods and his lazy wicked wife, life in the quiet hamlet of Hurst proves to be a daily challenge for Poppy, only softened by her caring neighbours who take it upon themselves to keep a watchful eye over her. A close and loving bond with the Greenfield family is formed over the years. Ella Greenfield is like a true sister, and a childhood love for Arthur Greenfield blossoms, but when relationships turn sour and Poppy feels forced to leave the only home she has ever known, a mysterious woman finds the perfect opportunity to step in. As the past catches up with the cold hearted Lady Hutchinson, the risk of her dark secrets being exposed determines her to once again take drastic action. How far is she prepared to go?

Yearning for a normal life and her true love, it is Poppy's inner strength and bravery which enhance her determined spirit.

The Whipple Girl

Toby Blake is a skilled con artist and a convincing liar. His overpowering desire to gain wealth and social standing at any price cast a devastating effect on the lives of his family, and anyone who crossed his path. His determination to better himself and make Helen Whipple his wife was only the beginning of a life of deception which left a tangle of lies behind him. When Helen's daughter was left to raise Toby Blake's only child under his strict and ruthless rule, Hester was determined to honour her mother's wish, and the promise she had made to her. Hester's strong love for her sister and the vow she had made to protect her from the evil ways of Toby Blake, meant a youth spent like a caged bird, desperate to find a way of escaping and of keeping her sister safe. Being forced to suddenly leave London for Oxford in 1873, Hester lost all contact with her only friend and childhood sweetheart, Harvey Gladstone, and as Toby Blake became trapped within his web of lies, he was prepared to take extreme measures, regardless of the consequences. How far was Toby Blake willing to go? Would Hester ever find freedom and her true love? A gripping tale of love, betrayal, and family loyalties.

Rose

Northamptonshire, 1865.
The callous Sebastian Harper returns home from a hunting trip on Bushel Farm with the devastating

news that his younger half-brother, Johnnie, has lost his life in a tragic accident. Sebastian has always believed that he should have been the sole inheritor of Bushel Farm when his father passed away, and now, with Johnnie out of the way, Sebastian is free to carry out his wicked plans for the future. With no love lost between himself and Johnnie, Sebastian is under the impression that he can simply take his half-brother's place and claim everything that belonged to him, including Rose, Johnnie's beautiful, young wife.

Rose is forced to take drastic actions and escape from Bushel Farm with her young son, Alfie, to a safe place, far from the ruthless Sebastian's evil clutches. With only a few shillings to her name and no relatives to shelter her, Rose's journey to freedom begins in the dark hours of night and marks the beginning of a series of events which will have a huge effect on the rest of her life.

Whitechapel Lass

Whitechapel, London, 1836 Born into poverty and hardship, and living in the filthy squalor of the tenement buildings, Ruby Skinner's decision to approach the unscrupulous East End villain, Donald McCoy, for help, ends in disaster. In a desperate bid to finance a move to rescue her ailing mother to the fresh air of the countryside, Ruby's plan does not go as expected, and she realises, too late, that she has made a huge mistake, which will consequently shape the rest of her life. Robert Thornton , a wealthy business man from the affluent area of Reigate, also had the misfortune of suffering from the under hand dealings with McCoy, and when curiosity forces him to pursue Ruby Skinner, the barriers which have always divided the social classes of the nineteenth century are put to test by the power of love. The thoroughly spoilt Clarissa Parker who has had her eyes set on Robert Thornton with the intention of becoming his wife, is not prepared to give him up easily, and with her malicious plans, sets out to destroy Ruby and Robert's happiness.When Ruby suddenly disappears, leaving behind her two year old daughter Victoria, Robert's search for her ends in vain, and leaves everyone to believe that she has somehow met with her death. Following in her mother's footsteps, nineteen years later, Victoria flees her home, to escape the unsuitable arranged marriage to the wealthy land owner George Stone. In his determined search for her, Robert's journey uncovers much more than he set out to find.

Daisy Grey

Set in the nineteenth century, ten-year-old Daisy Grey is delighted to be moving to Oxfordshire with her parents to start a new life. Daisy's father has at last found the perfect new home, in Lavender Farm, to rent, wanting nothing more than to farm the land and provide a decent life for his family, after living in a run-down cottage for years and struggling to earn a living as an odd job man. Although disappointed on arriving at Lavender Farm to find it not in the pristine condition that they'd been expecting, nothing could dampen the family's spirits, and Sam and Megan Grey, along with their daughter, set about restoring the run-down farm. After a dreadful tragedy occurs, shattering the entire family and leaving young Daisy in dire circumstances, it soon becomes apparent that the landlord and his wife have a darker side to them and Daisy becomes victim to their cruel plan. Daisy's life is marred by unfortunate circumstances and by her trepidation of the dreaded workhouse. When Daisy's path is crossed by a young homeless orphan from London, after she is forced to flee from her work in service, it marks the beginning of a friendship which finds them soon becoming inseparable. As Daisy is forced to quickly mature, her strong and dependable friendship with Alvin Clarke becomes bound by love. But life for the young couple is destined to change dramatically with the onset of the Crimean war.

Beneath The Apple Blossom Tree

Happily married to the rich and handsome Hugo Bowland of Redstone Lodge, Hannah is convinced that she has everything and more than she could ever wish for until the past finds its way back into her life and she becomes haunted by childhood memories and secrets.Beneath the apple blossom tree follows the early life of Hannah, a young girl who at only a few days old, was abandoned outside the orphanage in Little-Orangewood. Set in the nineteenth century the story tells of well kept hidden secrets and the heartache of forbidden love between the barriers of social divide. Rescued from the impoverished orphanage, Hannah is adopted and given a golden opportunity to live a full and privileged life, but it is not a life without heartbreak and emotional upheavals. When Hannah's beau, Gilbert King, mysteriously vanishes from the village of Little-Orangewood where he teaches at the local school, contrary to her adoptive father's beliefs, that he has merely endeavoured on a hasty escape to avoid any premature marriage commitments, Hannah is convinced that there is a more sinister reason behind his disappearance. A family bereavement and a chain of events forces Hannah and her family to leave the village to embark on a new and very different style of life. Now unable to pursue Gilbert's whereabouts, he is left to face his dire circumstances alone and loses all contact with his first love.A spiteful and younger orphan who becomes consumed with jealousy when a chance meeting brings her face to face with Hannah is determined to take revenge for the fact that she has not been given the same prosperous opportunities. Her unforgivable behaviour has detrimental and long-lasting effects on the lives of many. Will Hannah ever be free from her closely guarded secret and find true happiness again and will Gilbert King ever find true happiness again?

Faye

During one of the worst storms of November 1857, a young woman embarks on a desperate journey from London to Oxfordshire, hoping to reach the safety of her grandmother's home, where she grew up. In the relentless, torrential downpour and the gusty, chilling gales, the crippling pains of childbirth, force Faye Butler to deliver her heavy load on a soaked and muddy ditch by the side of the desolate highway. Exhausted, terrified, and completely alone, in the blackness of night, a baby girl enters the world.Meanwhile, as daybreak arrives after a disastrous evening in a London gentleman's club, Harry Fairbanks, a supposedly wealthy businessman is returning home to Harberton Mead House in Oxford. After losing virtually everything he owns at the gaming tables, he is left penniless and in debt.In a distraught state, and dreading having to break the news to his wife, Delia, of six years, his troubled mind prevents him from nodding off in his carriage and as dawn breaks, Harry suddenly catches sight of a discarded bonnet, fluttering in the wind upon a mound of mud. Ordering the coach driver to immediately halt, Harry Fairbanks is heartbroken by the harrowing scene which befalls him; a whimpering newborn, submerged in the cold muddy bog alongside her deceased mother.After rescuing the infant, and taking her home, Harry's life is made even more difficult when Delia and the staff at Harberton Mead become suspicious as to how Harry came upon the child. But, after succeeding to convince her that his story is the truth, Delia Fairbanks, who has yearned for her own child for many years, soon forms a strong attachment with baby Faye. In a desperate bid to try and recover some of his lost finances, Harry returns to the gaming tables of London where he becomes acquainted with Lyle Dagworth, who he finds in a state of melancholy. His eccentric wife, Marjorie Dagworth, who after seven months is still in full mourning over the tragic loss of her young baby, is driving him to despair and he fears for her sanity. When Harry discovers that Lyle Dagworth is a man of great wealth, he formulates a devious plan and offers Lyle the opportunity to purchase baby Faye.Whilst being entertained at Lyle Dagworth's impressive London home in Grosvenor Square, unknowingly to Harry, the bailiffs descend upon Harberton Mead and strip the house bare of its furniture and items of value, leaving Delia in a scornful rage. With the prolonged absence of Harry along with the threat that baby Faye will soon be taken from her and put into the workhouse, Delia decides that it is time to steer her life in a different direction and devote herself entirely to the precious baby who means the world to her. An intriguing, heartwarming novel with many unexpected twists and surprises. Guaranteed to tug on your heartstrings.

Secrets Of The Gatehouse

Childhood sweethearts, Silas Shepherd and his wife Claire have been happily married for sixteen years. Keeping with family tradition, they are tenant farmers, who reside on Squire, Reginald Brunswick's land in Bagley village with their son and three daughters. Although life in 1840 is often a struggle the family pride themselves on their unyielding unity and ability to cope with the hardships which befall them.With another baby on the way, Claire finds her proficiency to manage her family slowly ebbing away and fears she is losing control of her oldest children. While thirteen-year-old Martha Shepherd constantly has her head in the clouds, dreaming of an unrealistic future, Frank, is determined to prove he is no longer a boy and has made a solemn promise to himself to break with tradition and live a future life of wealth and prosperity, turning his back on what is expected of him, to follow in his father's footsteps. Prepared to break all the rules installed by his parents to accomplish his goals, Frank's rebellious actions soon initiate a series of catastrophic events.Bruce Brunswick, the Squire's mysterious, disfigured and crippled brother, resides at the gatehouse on the Brunswick Estate. Renowned for his eccentric and often sinister behaviour, he soon finds the opportunity to take advantage of Frank's rebellious ways as a means to threat and blackmail the Shepherd family, while at the same time, cover up his own immoral actions.With one disaster after another, the Shepherd family find themselves at their wit's end. Thrown into a state of turmoil they are forced to flee from their lifetime home to escape the looming threat and shameful scandal which surrounds them.Secrets of the gatehouse is a moving story about strong family ties and the enduring power of a family who is tested to their limits.The miracle of how love has the strength to change and influence characters is apparent throughout the story where twists and surprises are never far away.

Searching For Eleanor (Book One)

The sudden and untimely death of Eleanor Jackson's father, during the summer of eighteen seventy-five, brings to light a shocking revelation. For nearly fifteen years she has been kept in the dark, concerning her family's state of affairs. As Eleanor's privileged world comes tumbling down, she and her mother are destined for a life of poverty and hardship.A chance encounter with the handsome, August Miller initiates the beginning of a relationship, which has everlasting effects on both him and Eleanor, leaving them powerless to ignore the overwhelming surge of love, which has ignited in their hearts. When Eleanor's life is struck by yet another devastating tragedy, changing it dramatically, she becomes estranged from August and fearful of never setting eyes upon him again. August's unyielding adoration for Eleanor increases with every passing day, causing his life and the prospect of a life without her, to become unbearable. Resolute that he will never give up searching for her, August Miller is determined that one day, the beautiful, Eleanor will become his bride.Tortured by the disturbing knowledge that they might find themselves parted forever, 'Searching for Eleanor' is more than just a love story. It is a touching and often heartrending tale of adoration, faith and certainty. From a love kindled during the briefest of meetings, refusing to be extinguished by the passing of time or circumstance, this is the poignant story of two people whose hearts are as one, even through separation and trauma.

Loving August (Book Two)

The year is eighteen-seventy-eight and the benevolent Hyde family of Oxford is busy preparing for the long-awaited wedding between Eleanor Whitlock and August Miller. The strong sisterly bond which Eleanor and Tilly share has never wavered and they stand by their solemn vow, made during their time spent in the workhouse, to live as blood sisters for the rest of their lives. For the first time in many years, Tilly now has a sense of belonging and a valued position in life and feels confident and safe in her beliefs that nothing in the world could ruin her newly found happiness.

Meanwhile, in London's poverty-stricken, Whitechapel, Eleanor's malevolent half-sister, Rayne Jackson, is plotting ways in which she can jeopardize Eleanor's future joy. Convinced that August Miller is trapped in an unhappy relationship, Rayne's overpowering love for him, together with her refusal to believe that he harbours any genuine affection for Eleanor has increased her determination to continue in her pursuit of him.

When a sudden turn of events occurs, causing an unfavourable change to Rayne and her grandmother's welfare, suspicions are aroused by the arrival of the charismatic but dangerous, Buster Forbes. Keeping secret his past connection with his sworn enemy, the late Edward Jackson, Buster Forbes displays a generous and obliging nature towards Rayne and her grandmother, whilst biding his time before acting upon his dishonourable intentions.

Where will Rayne Jackson's dangerous scheme lead her? Will Eleanor and August ever achieve true happiness and how much is Tilly prepared to suffer for the sake of her beloved Eleanor?

Gracie's Pride

Situated in the heart of Cheshire, Hatherton Farm is a run-down, smallholding positioned on the Marshall's prestigious six-hundred-acre Estate. For three generations, a family feud has been the cause of misery and bitterness between the aristocratic Marshall family and the humble Browning family.
****

In eighteen fifty-one, the cruel and selfish, Joshua Browning sets sail from Liverpool to join the Californian gold rush, leaving his wife and twin sons behind, to run Hatherton Farm. Squire Cameron Marshall soon plots a way to regain the few acres of land, which he believes are rightfully his. Taking advantage of Gracie Browning's vulnerable situation, she soon finds herself exposed to lies and blackmail and at the mercy of the unscrupulous Squire. For the sake of her cherished sons, Gracie is compelled to make some huge and detrimental sacrifices.
****

With no alternative than to flee from their homeland, a terrible catastrophe inflicts a momentous and lasting change to the Browning family.
****

In their search for work and a new life, Oliver and Archie head towards London. During the journey,

Oliver meets a young farm girl which marks the beginning of a unique friendship. After suffering from her own personal loss, Sally Potts feels as though the hand of fate has thrown her and Oliver together, but their relationship is soon to be tested on a grand scale.

****

From Cheshire's scenic countryside, the distinguished outskirts of Oxford, and to the impoverished rookeries of London's East End; spread over thirty-three years and witnessing wealth and poverty, love, loss and betrayal and unexpected twists, Gracie's Pride is a gripping epic, guaranteed to intrigue and entertain.

Honeysuckle Bell

Although born and bred in the cosy hamlet of Sommerville Brook, it is not until Honeysuckle Bell is orphaned, in eighteen-thirty-six, at the age of twelve that she begins to realise how her late parents spent their entire lives as unwelcome tenants and were constantly ostracised by their hamlet neighbours.

On becoming Honeysuckle's guardian, Ruth Waldron seizes the opportunity to satisfy her vengeance, which has been eating away at her over the years. She demonstrates no kindness or compassion towards Honeysuckle, leaving her vowing to marry for wealth over love in her determination to seek the grander life that her late mother had always yearned for and to leave the sleepy hamlet when she matures.

Having been sheltered throughout her childhood, Honeysuckle is completely oblivious to the deep-rooted secrets and disturbing history between the Bell family and the Waldron family, until she stumbles across her mother's journal.

The discovery, along with the untimely eviction from Ruth Waldron's cottage, forces Honeysuckle on a hasty and premature journey in search of some answers.

Honeysuckle is a hamlet girl at heart and her desperate need to be part of a family often causes her amiable and affectionate nature to overpower what is best suited for her.

In her search for answers, Honeysuckle soon finds herself in a completely different world from the secure and peaceful hamlet and thrown amongst the poverty, disease and unscrupulous villains of London's East End.

Join Honeysuckle on her hazardous and often life-threatening journey from a girl to a young woman, where love is found in the most unexpected places and the truth is often deeply buried.

Printed in Great Britain
by Amazon